AMBUSH OR ADORE

BY GAIL CARRIGER

The Finishing School Series
Etiquette & Espionage
Curtsies & Conspiracies
Waistcoats & Weaponry
Manners & Mutiny

The Parasol Protectorate Series
Soulless
Changeless
Blameless
Heartless
Timeless

The Custard Protocol Series
Prudence
Imprudence
Competence
Reticence

Parasolverse Tie-in Books & Novellas
Poison or Protect
Defy or Defend
Ambush or Adore
Romancing the Werewolf
Romancing the Inventor
How to Marry a Werewolf

AS G. L. CARRIGER

A Tinkered Stars Mystery
The 5th Gender

The San Andreas Shifters Series
The Sumage Solution
The Omega Objection
The Enforcer Enigma

AMBUSH OR ADORE
A DELIGHTFULLY DEADLY NOVEL

GAIL CARRIGER

GAIL CARRIGER, LLC
This is a work of fiction. Names, characters, places, events, and incidents are either the product of the author's imagination, used in a fictitious manner, or in the public domain. Any resemblance to actual events or actual persons, living or dead, is coincidental.

WARNING
This work of fiction may contain sexually explicit situations of a romantic and carnal nature between members of the same sex, opposite sex, or both. If love (in its many forms) and love's consequences (in even more varied forms) are likely to offend, please do not read this book. Miss Carriger has a young adult quartet, the Finishing School series, that may be more to your taste. Thank you for your understanding, self-awareness, and self-control.

Copyright © 2021 by GAIL CARRIGER, LLC
Cover assembled by Starla Huchton, designedbystarla.com

The moral right of the author has been asserted.
ALL RIGHTS RESERVED, including the right to reproduce this book, or any portion thereof, in any form.
This book is for your personal enjoyment only. If you are reading this book and it was not purchased for your use, then please purchase your own copy.
In accordance with the U.S. Copyright Act of 1976, the uploading, torrenting, or electronic sharing of any part of this book without the permission of the publisher is unlawful piracy and theft of the author's intellectual property. If you would like to use material from the book (other than for review purposes), prior written permission must be obtained by contacting publisher@gailcarriger.com
The author strives to ensure her self-published works are available as widely as possible and at a price commensurate with her ability to earn a living. Thank you for respecting her hard work.

Version 1.0
ISBN 978-1-944751-33-3

gailcarriger.com

ACKNOWLEDGEMENTS

Thank you so much to my wonderful team. My amazing beta readers (Marie, Amber, Tanya, and Chanie) who caught all my mistakes, my awesome developmental editor Sue Brown-Moore (who deftly guided me through the mires of time spanning romance), my lovely copy editor Shelley Bates (who actually knows where the mysterious comma goes), and my amazing assistant Kelly without whom I truly would not function.

THE BEGINNING ENDS
SOGGY TOP HATS

Spring 1896 ~ Hyde Park, London

Pillover Plumleigh-Teignmott's biggest problem was that he met the love of his life when he was twelve years of age and then spent the rest of that life misplacing her.

Or more to the point, she kept intentionally misplacing herself.

If Pillover were to give love advice to anyone (which he wouldn't, because his expertise was in obscure ancient languages and certainly not love or, heaven forfend, romance) he'd tell them not to fall in love with a spy. Plays hell with one's heart, not to mention one's wardrobe and peace of mind.

Trying to hold onto an intelligencer was like grabbing for soap in a bathtub – very slippery and always causing a great deal of emotional splashing about that got everything wet and messy, but didn't ever really affect the soap. And one couldn't very well blame the soap, could one? After all, it's in its nature to slip away, again and again.

Pillover had thought this thought for the very first time years ago, when he'd swished his skirts around uncomfortably at a school for evil geniuses. At the time, he'd been tasked with providing a distraction, and very effective those skirts turned out to be, if he did say so himself. And he thought this thought again over forty years later, when he went to meet a dirigible in the middle of a rainstorm on the off chance that his lady-love might, just maybe, be aboard.

This last time Pillover had misplaced her for well over a year (longer than ever before). He worried maybe he'd missed the chance to tell her the stupid, tiny, insignificant detail of his heart being caught up in her red hair like a floundering fish in a net. Because that was the other thing about spies – sometimes when they disappeared, they disappeared forever.

It's possible that Pillover had never told Agatha of his love because his metaphors were pants and he was no poet to know the right words. But it would, in fact, be beyond silly to have held his reserve for decades only to have her die on him, misplaced forever. That would be worse than careless. That would be sloppy.

Back to the fact that being in love with a spy was slippery and hell on the wardrobe.

It was raining, hard. Pillover's top hat was soggy and collapsing slightly on one side. His suit was made of that kind of fabric (his sister would know the name) that showed every single drop as a dark stain, with no greatcoat to protect him. He'd forgotten it somewhere. Because who would have thought it might rain in early spring in London? (Everyone but Pillover, naturally.) Consequently, he didn't look as he ought, waiting for the light of his life with the certain knowledge that he had, in order to save her, also betrayed her trust. He wasn't sure why he was there at all. Simply to see her again as soon as possible? To beg forgiveness?

Regardless, he did not make a very prepossessing figure, which was probably a good thing. Agatha never liked a scene. It was unlikely she wanted him there at all, especially after he'd shared the photograph. Plus she hated being noticed. Which meant she preferred it when he faded into the background, too. Pillover was only tolerably good at that, an unfortunate accident of genetics having made him rather more handsome than he was comfortable with.

There had been a phase, once, when ladies found his sulky air combined with dark good looks appealing. That inevitably passed when he responded with little to no conversation or encouragement. Now, while most of his hair was still holding on valiantly, it was going grey. His shoulders were stooped from bending over manuscripts, his face wrinkled from squinting in weak lighting. He had to wear spectacles all the time instead of just for reading. He looked, in fact, exactly as he was, an Oxford don of middling teaching capacity but good reputation, well published and set in his ways – a confirmed bachelor. His sulky air was now deemed grumpy and eccentric. His lack of a wife termed *a crying shame* and regarded by the artistic set with raised eyebrows. His continued occupancy of a cozy cottage alone in Oxford was thought slightly suspicious. Why did an Oxford man of Pillover's tenure and disposition need to keep a house alone? And what need had he to visit London when there were no symposia on offer? What secrets did he keep that led him to pursue such a solitary lifestyle, and did they involve mistresses or molly houses or something more sinister?

On a landing green in Hyde Park, in the pouring rain, did Pillover look like a man waiting for the love of his life?

As he had always waited. As he'd probably continue to wait even if she had misplaced herself permanently.

It was worse, he thought, to be the one who waited than the one who went away. She always knew what was happening to her when it was happening. He had to guess and imagine and hope she returned. Perhaps some of the curve in his shoulders and the grey in his hair was payment paid to the consequences of misplaced affection.

Pillover had never attained the rank of Evil Genius. He'd only gotten as far as Reprobate Genius, but when it came to Agatha he sometimes thought even the *genius* part was a misnomer. He, who had translated Catullus. He, who had his research on Roman linguistic variance as relates to Linear B accepted for publication by no fewer than six academic societies. He, Pillover, could not fathom or comprehend one redheaded female. And he never had.

~

Spring 1896 ~ Spotted Custard dirigible, somewhere in the aetherosphere en route back to London

Agatha never bothered to ask the *Spotted Custard*'s crew how Sophronia knew where to direct them to find her. She figured there were coils within coils and if one needed to track an intelligencer then the smartest choice was to find another intelligencer to do so. Sophronia, being Sophronia, had *delegated*. The end result was that Agatha, who had never needed nor asked for anyone's help, had been pulled out of the soup by the most eccentric crew of misfits she'd ever encountered in her life. And she'd been a spy for fully four decades.

Suffice it to say, *ordinarily* Miss Agatha Woosmoss

would certainly not have required their assistance. *Ordinarily* they wouldn't have been able to find her, either. Agatha was usually good at covering any traces of her presence. However, when someone else got hold of her, they were not so good at hiding it.

That had happened too many times on this particular run. First in India, then in Singapore, and then in the Paper City. A terrible string of bad luck plus the necessary destruction of her only means of escape, and Agatha had ended up having to take shelter with the very creatures she'd come to Japan to find – fox shifters. She was convinced Lord Akeldama would never forgive her for it, but was also tolerably certain she didn't care anymore for the vampire's good opinion. She'd taken a certain visceral pleasure in the company of the kitsune. They were creatures of power and connection. They were bossy women making trickster choices with crafty intent. They reminded her in many ways of her dearest friends, Sophronia, Dimity, Sidheag, and Vieve. Not as they were now, but their schoolgirl selves. As if there were an element of childish whimsy to fox shifters, although kitsune were reputed to be some of the oldest shifters on earth.

Maybe Agatha had stayed a little too long with them because of this. And maybe that was part of it – around kitsune one lost track of time.

Yet what Sophronia chose to send and pull Agatha out of Japan with was, quite frankly, ridiculous. A fancy modernized pleasure dirigible that looked like a massive ladybug captained by Lord Akeldama's spoiled adopted daughter and crewed by her ridiculous friends? The audacity of it all! Agatha identified Vieve's son and one of Vieve's assets in the boiler room. There was Preshea's daughter in the swoon room. Not to mention a set of twins who were somehow related to Sophronia. And of course, there was another of Lord Akeldama's spies aboard already. He would never let his daughter out of his sight for long without a watcher. The ship was crawling with legacy intelligencers. Blundering, awkward, untrained, unsubtle children, so far as Agatha was concerned. But who was she to judge the exhausting representatives of new youth?

Of course she judged. Spying was her only passion and her entire business.

They'd created a rollicking mess, of course. Exposed her, her position, and the kitsune in the process. Even started a mini-revolution and certainly instigated massive civil unrest, because Prudence Akeldama was not an asset, she was a blunt instrument of chaos. Agatha thought it mildly unfair of Lord Akeldama to have unleashed her on the world. Not to mention Sophronia's activating her. What she failed to realize was that someone else had activated Sophronia.

Still, Agatha was unexpectedly happy to be heading home. It was a sensation she so rarely enjoyed, and it was colored by a certain confidence in two things – that she was going to leave her patron and that she was about to take a whole new kind of risk.

It made her, on the grey shrouded deck of a fancy dirigible coasting the aether currents with deceptive speed, oddly nostalgic.

CHAPTER ONE
NO ONE FORGETS THEIR FIRST VAMPIRE

1848 ~ London

Agatha Woosmoss was ten years old when she met her first vampire. He would not be her last. But he would be the most important for the rest of her life.

She was to learn during the course of their association that Lord Akeldama was like that. And she *had* to learn how to forgive him for being fabulous and somehow vital in her life despite her best efforts to the contrary. Vampire fangs were the fulcrum upon which society pivoted. Lord Akeldama's fangs were sharper and more present than most.

When he'd first found her, she'd been hiding. That alone would have told her he was different, special. Normally when Agatha was hiding, no one could find her. No one wanted to. But the strange vampire turned out to be important and perceptive in a way that other grownups normally were not. The way he moved was unusual, too. It was as if his body knew that it could (and should) go faster than it did, all the time, but was muffling itself. As if his whole gorgeous, brazen appearance was actually a physical whisper – subverted so as not to be a threat.

Agatha, age ten, was very good at identifying threats.

"What are you doing here, little girl child?" he asked, sliding behind the curtain next to her.

With which action he went from being the center of everyone's focus to being lost and invisible, just like her. Agatha was deeply impressed, and she wanted to know how he did it.

"I'm watching, sir."

"Are you, indeed, *little* button? And what have you learned?"

"I will tell you if you will tell me how you knew I was here."

The flash of his fangs was a surprise to both of them. "Bargaining already? Very well. Some of us only watch the shadows – the light can take care of itself."

She nodded. It was one of those adult non-answers. She was accustomed to those. But she could play them back at him, if he wanted that kind of music.

"I have seen two possible affaires of the heart, a missing diamond ring, the one who drinks too much, and the one who drinks too little. I have seen the fire of too much avarice and the pride of too little consequence. It is the same as all of Papa's other parties, and yet not, because you are here with your fancy men – all flash and bother and trained to see everything. Do you wish to compare notes?" She was proud of her barbs.

Agatha thought, if he let himself, the vampire might look impressed. "How old are you, *toggles*?"

"Old enough to know I should look for the unsaid things first."

AMBUSH OR ADORE

He tilted his head and eyed her neck but not, she thought, with real interest. Vampires did not recruit children. It was one of their most sacred rules. She thought maybe he was wondering if she were worth raising up to adulthood, like livestock. So he might recruit her when she was grown. She wondered if she would end up a cow for him to milk, or veal pie?

"Do you have a *patron*?" he asked.

Agatha actually laughed at him. Then quickly suppressed the sound. She wanted to stay hidden even if she must share the shadows.

"I am only ten, my lord."

"Only that? Still an infant, then. I am terrible at guessing human ages. You all look young to me. What's your name, baby bean?"

"Agatha Woosmoss, sir."

"Of course it is. How would you like to do this forever?"

"Do what, exactly?"

"Hide and watch."

Agatha thought it sounded nice, but two years ago she had enjoyed playing with a porcelain goose doll dressed like a strawberry. Tastes changed. "Does anyone know, at ten, what they want to do for the rest of their life?"

"I don't understand how humans think. You only have one short life to live. Why not spend it on something you're actually good at?"

Agatha frowned and considered. "I want to be free. Can you give me that?" She gestured at the party with all its games of society, and marriage, and restrictions – the tiny, boring life offered to girls like her.

"You would be trapped by me. But everyone else, no."

Agatha wondered if trading freedom futures was something vampires did regularly. Probably. "But you are bound by your own code, are you not?"

"Isn't everyone?"

Agatha thought about her mild-mannered mother, plain and round and quietly bruised. She had lived a life in timidity and fear and died the same way. No ghost came from her. Her soul had been squeezed dry by a life of insignificance until she'd had nothing left worth leaving behind.

Agatha was old enough to realize how young she really was, but she knew one thing for certain – she did not want to live a life of inconsequence and neglect.

Of course, she did not know then that she was trading that future for one where she intentionally neglected the world instead. As if, in an effort not to be worthless, she would withdraw from everything, even reality. She would turn everything that had made her mother weak into her own strengths.

But in that moment, talking to a vampire behind the heavy velvet curtains of a too-expensive house at a too-indulgent party, she made the choice anyway.

"To be truly lazy, one chooses eternal life, no?"

The vampire laughed. "Touché, my little *wallflower*. Touché. I don't normally recruit females. How very strange a creature you are."

"I do not want to be your drone."

"You don't? Give yourself time. Youth always thinks itself eternal. In forty years, perhaps you will change your mind."

Agatha considered the possibility of wanting to be a vampire. "I don't believe so, but ask me again then. We shall see how much my character has altered by the time I'm fifty." It turned out that this was a sentiment she would never regret and never change. One of the few.

"Do you believe you have excess soul, little *button*?" The vampire gave her an up-and-down assessment.

Agatha knew exactly what he saw. A plain girl, dowdy, regretfully redheaded and freckled, with a demeanor that was quiet, mild mannered, and invisible. There was nothing special or creative or excess about Agatha. She had nothing to carry her over into immortality and she knew it.

"Probably not, but that doesn't make me worthless."

"It does to most vampires."

"And yet here you stand, my lord, talking secretly to a ten-year-old girl at a party. Are you rescinding your offer already?"

He chuckled. "I'm not most vampires and you're funny. I didn't think a child could be so diverting. It's refreshing. Very well, I will see this done – as your patron, but not your master. Have you ever wanted to attend *finishing school*?"

"No."

"Change your mind."

"If you insist, my lord." Suddenly, she liked him. He was full of plots.

"I will have one of my drones mention the name of one particularly *interesting* educational institution to your father. I will arrange to pay the fees and keep you in funds and attire. You will report to me what you learn there. And I do *not* mean the *lessons*. I mean the information that flows through the teachers and students. It is a very well *connected* school and you will emerge well connected and well educated because of it."

"Finishing school, my lord?"

"The kind that teaches you how to *finish* everything, and not just your supper."

"Even vampires?"

"Especially vampires. However, you are to avoid

attracting any kind of attention whilst you are there, even from vampires. Especially from us."

"I will endeavor to be the best while pretending to be the worst."

"I have no doubt."

Without sparing her another glance, Lord Akeldama slid out from behind the curtains. He became once more the darling of the assembled, the prince of witty repartee, and the object of many adoring eyes.

Agatha had bargained with a monster at age ten. He wore sunset purple satin and gold lace, and he would be her closest ally for the rest of her life. Perhaps it was a devil's pact or perhaps it was a gentleman's agreement. Since Agatha was neither gentleman nor devil, she would only learn the price much, much later.

Decades later, she would calculate the cost on the deck of a fancy dirigible shaped like a ladybug and crewed by eccentrics. She would think of that payment not in terms of the scars she bore and the blood she'd risked and lost, as a vampire might, but in terms of her disaffected heart. That one thing she'd held too hard in reserve and never risked at all.

But still, she would never regret the bargain she'd struck.

She began attending finishing school three years later.

∽

Pillover Plumleigh-Teignmott, on the other hand, did not remember his first vampire at all. Unlike Agatha, he'd never had a defining moment of clarity connected to the supernatural set. He had been mildly annoyed when a vampire queen kidnapped him. But even that hadn't had a profound impact on his life in the long run. He'd grown up around vampires, werewolves, and their sycophants. His parents, being evil geniuses, dealt with the supernatural set on the regular. There were always drones and clavigers coming and going from their country house. At various times the family would take residence in one of the lesser known but more refined neighborhoods. Then, there had been vampires. Pillover had confessed to Agatha once that he felt that he *ought* to have remembered his first. But he'd been too young.

His parents had dealt with the inconvenience of children by carting them everywhere and mostly ignoring them. This left Pillover and his sister to entertain each other. Which, as he was the younger, mostly meant his sister dressing him up and treating him like a living doll. This might have turned an ordinary schoolboy evil, but Pillover hadn't really minded, and perhaps this made him more sympathetic to vampire drones than most. It did, however, give him a near virulent disregard for fashion. As much as his sister loved fripperies and fobs, he was disposed to dislike them intensely.

When Pillover was shipped away to school at eleven years old, he was in his oversized bowler and oiled greatcoat stage. He had spectacles that were very thick, a brow that was very creased, and a large, dusty book normally occupying the entirety of his lap and attention. This persona had allowed him to resist his sister's efforts of late and remain ignored by his parents. But it served him ill at Bunson and Lacroix's Boys' Polytechnique.

In short, he arrived at evil genius training academy already younger than most of the students, and instantly became the preferred whipping boy for anyone who thought they were better than he. Which, as it turned out, was most everyone else at Bunson and Lacroix's Boys' Polytechnique.

It was a cruel thing his parents had done, sending him to an evil genius school. But as they were both evil geniuses themselves, he ought to have been better prepared. Perhaps Pillover should have paid more attention to those vampires – they were supposed to be some of the best at being evil. His father was a founding member of the Death Weasel Confederacy, and his mother was a kitchen chemist of questionable intent, but Pillover was just bad at being bad. He had the genius bit in hand (well, he did if you asked him about it) but he was not and never would be at all good at being evil. Which meant, of course, that everyone else got to practice their evil on him.

The Pistons made his life at school particularly horrid. Strutting about in riding boots and black blouses, sewing cogs onto their outfits in a non-useful manner. (This last affectation was particularly egregious so far as Pill was concerned. Not that he was a mechanic or an engineer, but it was just so wasteful.) The Pistons used their aristocratic connections and their club rules as an excuse to push him around. Apparently only Pillover believed they attended school to *learn* things.

Fortunately, he only had to survive eight years of it.

Eight years.

And then they introduced girls into the mix.

It was absolutely awful. A tragedy.

~

Autumn 1851 ~ Mademoiselle Geraldine's Finishing Academy for Young Ladies of Quality, somewhere over Devon

Agatha would have survived finishing school no matter what, but much to her surprise, she made friends. And friends, it turned out, made everything that much easier. The teachers were strict, the classes were hard, and most of the girls were both pretty and pretty darned mean. But, so far as Agatha was concerned, anything was better than her father's household, and she would do whatever she could never to return.

The friends were unexpected. In many ways an added burden, as she had to lie to them, too, while sending her regular reports back to Lord Akeldama. She tried not to have to do it too much, and she tried to be as genuine and kind as possible. They were, after all, at a school for spies and assassins – intelligencers. She hoped that they would forgive her a minor, if extensive, double crossing.

She ended up liking her friends quite a bit. And, much to her shock and amazement, they seemed to like her back. Sidheag was the first to win her over. Agatha was grateful they'd been told to share a room, for it was the Lady of Kingair who introduced her to the others. Tall, grumpy, and Scottish, Sidheag Maccon came off as gruff, but turned out to be kindly underneath it all. Sidheag saw none of the usual flaws in Agatha's timid manner, dumpy appearance, or awkward address, because Sidheag saw only actions, and Agatha was never cruel. In fact, Agatha never did anything to attract any kind of attention at all. She knew where her talents lay. And while Sidheag never noticed the intent, she actually really liked that Agatha was a wallflower.

After Sidheag came Sophronia – proud and cunning and a little bit scary. After Sophronia came Vieve – tiny, fierce, and irrepressibly mechanically minded. Trailing Sophronia, like a very sparkly puppy, was Dimity, the easiest to like of them all. Dimity was chattery and sweet. Agatha worried about her sometimes. Because her parents might be evil, but Dimity had inherited none of it.

Finally, after Dimity, came her younger brother,

Pillover. He turned out to be even softer than his sister, so Agatha worried about him most of all. He was a brilliant, sullen boy, full of sarcasm and concern. Complaining even as he always helped, no matter the cost to his own life and personal preferences. He was a lumpy bundle of grumpy loyalty that Agatha felt none of them really deserved, least of all herself. Yet he gave them all equal parts annoyance and affection, unreservedly, as if he had no choice. As if he felt they were worthy merely by virtue of being his sister's companions.

Sophronia basically conscripted Pillover into her — and consequently *their* — shenanigans by default, and then kept him around because she found him useful. Sophronia found odd people useful. Agatha didn't meet Pillover right away. After all, they were in a girls' school floating about the clouds, and he was at a boys' school in a secret location far below. But Agatha did hear about him on those rare occasions when Dimity was moved to talk about family. Which wasn't often. Having no siblings of her own, Agatha couldn't sympathize with Dimity's complaints about her "pustule of a brother," but she could *imagine* the frustration.

When Agatha did meet Pillover, she very much liked him from the start — glum but restful, and quietly smart about Latin, if not people. Agatha didn't learn Latin, but she appreciated a boy who obsessed over something so obscure. She thought it showed strength of character not to be taken in, like the Pistons, by rank and appearances, but instead to be taken in by the secret knowledge of an ancient world. After all, she had been taken in by the secret knowledge of this one.

Not that her liking him mattered all that much.

Not at first, anyway.

∽

Pillover got occasional notes from his appalling sister for the first six months of school. They came sporadically because mail had to wait until her school floated close to some acceptably rural village or other. He did not hear from his parents. They weren't the floating types and had nowhere near his sister's excuse, but they were probably distracted by corrosive capybara carcasses or something equally vile.

Pillover would never admit that he looked forward to Dimity's funny sideways rambling, but he did. He read about her new friends. She was the type to make friends easily. He wasn't convinced that he envied her that. Apparently her friends numbered only three, so she wasn't *that* good. He'd met Sophronia, who was very smart and good fun (according to Dimity) but whom Pillover had found rather brash and excitable. Sophronia was the type of forward female who enjoyed adventure and physical action, both of which Pillover deeply mistrusted and somewhat feared. Still, he didn't have to put up with her, Dimity did.

Dimity wrote of others – someone named Sidheag who was Scottish and had been raised by wolves (which Dimity found exciting but also rather scandalous), and another one named Agatha. What Dimity had to say about Agatha could be summed up in four lines of text.

My new friend Agatha is sweet and gentle, but I worry about her because she lacks sparkle. Our school is not a good place for such a person. She is also somewhat shy. If she is to last, we must look after her.

Pillover therefore liked Agatha best of Dimity's friends well before he actually met her (purely on the grounds of four lines in his sister's rather flowery prose). But that was all he knew of her until the following term.

Pillover never dreamed he'd get to see the inside of his sister's school. It was, after all, a massive floating dirigible for *girls alone*. Yet, eventually he found himself wandering the halls of Mademoiselle Geraldine's Finishing Academy for Young Ladies of Quality, confused about life. Of course, he was newly thirteen years of age, so he was always confused about life. But this made things worse, to be one of only ten boys surrounded by girls. Surrounded by the enemy. They were there for a trip, a special treat. And he'd been included only because he had a sister on board. (Or so he'd thought.) It was supposed to be a *good* thing. A reward. Floating along with all those girls on a special jaunt into London on a massive dirigible.

Pillover hated London.

Pillover did *not* like girls.

And frankly, he wasn't sold on dirigibles, either.

He remembered only snippets of that first visit. The way the lighting overhead looked like parasols. How still the school was – it didn't feel like it was floating at all, but it also didn't feel like it was grounded.

Pillover thought that memories were like dust motes of time. They inhabited the air around him but he never noticed them unless the sunlight struck just right, or they made him sneeze. Most of his years at school were long since dissipated into the aether, moted and hazy. But sometimes, some bit would sparkle just so and he would find himself sneezing with memory.

He recalled perfectly what it felt like to walk into the dining hall and see the faces of *so many* girls staring at him. Pretty, eager, chatty females craning their necks and staring at him, like a massive flock of multicolored flamingos at tea. Deadly flamingos. Pillover found every part of the situation terrifying, even the tea.

Except that he, and he alone, had familiar faces to search for. There was his sister. And there was Sophronia. And there next to Dimity sat a slumped, frightened-looking girl with red hair whom Pillover guessed was Agatha. She looked even more frightened than he felt, which was oddly comforting.

Not everyone is lucky enough to remember their first impressions. But Pillover never forgot Agatha's frightened face. Possibly because years later he would realize how false a face it had been. Would become afraid that his first impression of the love of his life had been entirely fake. Or had it? That was the game his brain played on him where Agatha was concerned. Questionable memories were parceled up with her questionable identity.

They were all undertaking a trip to London. Pillover was assigned to the dining table with Sophronia for the duration. She was a good egg whom he liked, insofar as one could like a girl and think of her as in any way eggish. In her usual fashion, Sophronia had him under her wing and doing several odd things after only a few days aboard (including writing to his *parents* because she thought someone was threatening his sister). Ordinarily Pillover would have been disposed to think of this as feminine hysteria, but not with Sophronia. Not that he was inclined to argue or disobey her instructions – no point, Sophronia would win regardless. She was like that. Girls were, frankly, in general like that. Pillover supposed he was destined to be one of those gentlemen entirely ruled by his wife. He considered this, and then resigned himself to his fate and stuffed his face with better food while he could.

They did have superior comestibles aboard the dirigible. Bunson's meals were notoriously bad, as though the food were also trying to be evil, but Geraldine's girls enjoyed a varied and respectable diet. Partly because they were supposed to learn all the appropriate cutlery and etiquette for every possible cuisine, and partly so they could taste the various flavors and work to understand which poisons were best hidden in what dishes.

His sister was in some kind of mood through most of the trip, ignoring both him and Sophronia, which Pillover took as a godsend. He left it up to Sophronia to figure out what was going on and simply tried to survive the sea of indistinguishable, terrifying femininity. There was a kind of evil to girls that even he, at a school for the stuff, couldn't fully comprehend. A circulation of carefully calculated compliments that weren't and small, petty digs with huge significance. He found everything about it exhausting.

Eventually, Dimity and Sophronia made up their differences and Pillover found himself spending the remainder of the trip in the bosom of his sister's friendships. He got to meet Sidheag, who was pleasingly brash and unrefined, but regrettably Scottish. He rather preferred his languages dead and not complicating current-day vocabulary. He wasn't even confident in English, which seemed a messy sort of barbarian language, always stealing from others. And then, of course, Agatha.

Agatha never chattered. Pillover considered chattiness the worst flaw in a girl, so her quietness was beautiful. Agatha seemed to enjoy fading into the background, an instinct Pillover understood all too well. But it made him want to watch her more than the others.

A lot happened on that trip. He even got kidnapped by vampires – messy business. A lot that he forgot and only bits of which he could recall given the right incentives. Memory was a funny old thing. But what he recalled most clearly was dancing with Agatha for the first time.

He remembered how restful she was compared to his other partners. She didn't try to talk. If he mentioned something Latin, she never acted confused or overly interested – just nodded. She was taller than he back then, a worldly fifteen to his thirteen. He remembered that she felt graceful in his arms, as if she were going easy on him. He thought that maybe her clumsy gawkiness with other partners was a sham and he wondered why. He considered asking her, but felt that would be intrusive. So instead he just enjoyed that she was round and soft and that she didn't say anything except with her eyes. They were big and a kind of watery greenish color, like a pot he'd seen once in a museum. Celadon, it was called. He thought they were also sad. Pillover, who spent most of his time being intentionally morose, rather admired a winsome misery in others. He wanted to ask her what was wrong. But he never did.

He never would.

Pillover returned unharmed to Bunson's (despite the vampires' best efforts) with a weird ache in his throat whenever he thought about his sister's redheaded companion. He also had a friend at last – a new evil genius student in the form of a girl pretending to be a boy. He got to help young Vieve disguise herself and infiltrate Bunson's. It was fun, and he finally had a companion at school, but also it was evil to hide a girl from his professors, and he'd yet to do anything truly evil. He figured that if he were found out, he'd get top marks.

Under normal circumstances, were they not evil geniuses and lady spies, Pillover's first stirring of childish interest would have been doomed and deadened by distance and time. It would all have ended with that first dance. But Geraldine's and Bunson's were reverse sides of the same coin – tarnished and dented, but constantly flipping. He would see Agatha again and again over the years even after school had ended (or in the case of Geraldine's, crashed) because it turned out that the friendship of girls was a strong and steady thing. Dimity would remain close to

Agatha their whole lives, even after Agatha's betrayal (maybe partly because of it).

And Pillover?

Well, Pillover was regrettably steady in all his interests. He was a creature of habit. He never gave up puzzling out the nuances of Latin verse, and he never gave up trying to understand the sadness in those celadon eyes.

CHAPTER TWO

SWATH CUTTING AND OTHER CONCERNS

February 1853 ~ Mademoiselle Geraldine's Finishing Academy for Young Ladies of Quality, somewhere over Devon

Sophronia and Dimity were ribbing Sidheag about her obvious interest in Captain Niall and Agatha could not bear it. It was too humiliating to be teased about something romantic. It made her think about Pillover, whom she hadn't seen in ages and which was terribly inappropriate given their age difference and social standing. She pushed the thought of him aside and really wished she could come up with a means of stopping the conversation in front of her.

Sidheag, of course, was well able to defend herself. "He's ten times my age!"

Dimity was like a mouse with a tasty biscuit. "Immortals often are. He still cuts a fine figure."

It made Agatha feel hot. Surely not?

Sophronia pressed. "And you know werewolves, Sid. I mean to say, you *know* them."

Sidheag, who was ordinarily stalwart, actually blushed at this.

Agatha was moved to intercede at last. She did it by returning them to the subject of preparing for class. "I've misplaced my chewing tobacco for informant recruiting."

"Again? Really, Agatha." Her tactic worked, as Sidheag forgot her embarrassment in annoyance at Agatha's near constant missteps.

Agatha pretended to bristle. "Yesterday's lip tint dematerialization was due to the chaotic mess that is your side of the room."

"You canna blame me for your absent-mindedness." Sidheag was gruff.

"Yes, I can." Agatha only really allowed herself gumption with Sidheag. With everyone else, she let her own natural timidity lead. But after living with Sidheag for a while now, she'd had to stick up for herself occasionally or she got railroaded all the time. It worked, because Sidheag was secretly a big softy. They now existed in a state of bickering equilibrium that was as close to that of siblings as Agatha would ever get. Mindful of Lord Akeldama's instructions, she only allowed herself the luxury of a backbone with Sidheag.

Preshea wandered over. Agatha watched her approach, but the others were taken unawares when the girl spoke. "Are you going to sit there gossiping all night?"

The dining room had emptied out and the mechanicals were clearing the tables.

Preshea's voice took on the sickly-sweet tone that indicated she was about to say something mean. Agatha braced herself, since these barbs were often directed at her. She had set herself up as the weakest link and easy victim of the school. She didn't mind – it deflected attention from the others. And it made her look unthreatening. Always unthreatening. If she couldn't be invisible, unthreatening was the next best thing.

Preshea's clipped voice said, "Are you going to gather up the abandoned pikelets so that Agatha can eat them all later?"

This was a dig at her chubby frame and Agatha could not deny that it hurt. She let herself tear up.

Sidheag, no great wit, could come up with no rebuttal, but being Sidheag (a woman of action) she threw her uneaten pikelet at Preshea.

Preshea was shocked. "Lady Kingair, this is a new gown!"

"Then dinna go around being nasty when some of us are armed with nibbly bits." Sidheag was unrepentant.

Agatha stifled a smile. She did love Sidheag so.

Preshea flounced away like an affronted titmouse.

Dimity patted Agatha's shoulder softly. "Ignore her. That girl is walking, talking indigestion." She turned to her best friend. "Sophronia, isn't there something we could *do* about her?"

Agatha was curious as to Sophronia's response. As she had told Lord Akeldama, Sophronia had a natural talent for spycraft, and not just intelligence gathering, but also human manipulation. Sophronia not only saw the wheels in motion, she saw the road they traveled on and sometimes, she could change the direction of the trolley. Sophronia might become a very good intelligencer, perhaps one of the best, except that she was cursed with a code of ethics. Agatha recognized her own limits in that she would only ever be an observer of history, never an influencer. But as Lord Akeldama wrote back, observers were useful in their own right. So Agatha didn't feel too bad about it.

Sophronia considered Dimity's suggestion. "I don't

know if it's worth the risk. The teachers have been watching me since the Westminster Hive incident."

Agatha didn't like to think about that. Pillover had been kidnapped as well as Dimity. Poor Pillover wouldn't say boo to a goose. He didn't deserve to be in danger. He didn't deserve to be involved. He didn't deserve vampires. Agatha had had rather strong words to say to Lord Akeldama on the subject – after all, his kind had been at fault. Lord Akeldama hadn't apologized. He never apologized. But she thought maybe he understood. And, hopefully, it wouldn't happen again.

She remembered being startled by the strength of her own anger. As if Pillover's being taken was a personal affront. She had been almost vampirelike in her possession of him. Perhaps she had already spent too much time with Lord Akeldama, that his idea of affection had transmitted to her. Or perhaps, even then, it had already been love. Her greatest failing all along, that she recognized love in others but never in herself. No wonder it had come to the surface of the child she was, as possession and anger.

They abandoned the last of the pikelets and did not, in fact, keep them for snacks. They were heading towards their next class when they were waylaid by Professor Lefoux, the most fearsome teacher at the school.

She stood blocking Sidheag's way. "Lady Kingair, you have received a pigeon."

Agatha gasped. Pigeons were a serious business. They were for emergency use only.

Sidheag began asking questions about her family – the werewolf pack back home, were they safe? Professor Lefoux clearly felt this was a private matter and led Sidheag away before answering.

Dimity spoke into the ensuing silence. "This is bad. What could possibly require pigeoning?"

AMBUSH OR ADORE

Agatha exchanged glances with Sophronia. It must be werewolf business, which meant Lord Akeldama would want to know. She'd have to ask Sidheag about it later. Also, she cared for her friend and wanted to do what she could to help if possible. She wasn't a monster.

Sophronia got it, of course. "Must be problems with the pack. Only a crisis in the supernatural community warrants *the pigeon*."

Agatha nodded.

"We're going to miss class if we keep speculating and that won't help matters." Sophronia hustled them onwards.

Later that day, Sidheag ended up consulting Captain Niall about the missive, not her friends, which meant the pigeon had either come from or pertained to werewolves.

Agatha asked Sidheag about it that night, when it was just the two of them in their sleeping chamber together.

"Sid, that pigeon you got – is your pack well?"

"It's private werewolf business. I canna talk about it," Sidheag practically snapped.

Agatha immediately backed down. "Of course, I don't mean to pry. I hope you know that if you confided in me, I would never tell." The lie came too easily.

"I know that, Ags." Poor Sidheag. She was gullible – definitely not cut out to last long at their school.

Agatha really was only asking out of friendship. She had already managed to extract, read, and return the missive to Sidheag's hiding place. That very night after Sidheag fell asleep, Agatha intended to write of it to Lord Akeldama. He needed to know that the Kingair pack was treasonous. She wasn't sure whether her vampire patron would act on this information. To be fair, she wasn't certain what, if anything, he did with any of the information she provided. Or what he did in general, for that matter. But he would praise her by return post, and most of the time that was all she really needed. Along with her allowance and the freedom it afforded her, of course. But the praise, it was something Agatha had come to yearn for. She was frightened by how much. No one had ever praised her for anything. Yet this one fancy vampire prince-god thought she was wonderful just because she was good at exactly the thing she'd been pilloried for all her childhood. It was heady – to be admired for one's flaws.

Sidheag softened enough to explain. "I don't want to worry you. And what advice could you possibly offer concerning werewolves?"

Agatha let her face fall and nodded. "True. But I can be a sympathetic ear."

Sidheag threw a long, bony arm about her shoulders and squeezed a little too hard. "Dinna fret yourself. 'Twill all be fine in the end." Her brogue came through almost as strongly as her concern.

Agatha wondered if she would ever become accustomed to the sickly feeling of having to betray her closest friends.

Sidheag would vanish shortly thereafter to parts unknown and Agatha would miss her friend very much, but she would not miss the need for betrayal.

∼

Something changed during the course of that year. What Pillover remembered most was being hungry all the time. As if in response to this memory, his stomach growled. Now he was standing in the rain, nostalgic, top hat soggy beyond redemption, and hungry to boot.

"You're experiencing unprecedented growth," Vieve had said at the time (he no longer had that excuse). It had sounded hilarious coming in a French accent from a diminutive girl dressed as a boy.

Pillover hid a smile. "You make it sound as if I were a speculative investment of some ilk. Dirigible, perhaps."

Vieve frowned. "You should eat liver. Liver is just the thing for unprecedented growth."

Pillover wrinkled his nose. "I'd rather go hungry, thank you very much."

"Only trying to help."

"Well, stop it." Pillover's voice had started to crack and drop. He'd had to learn to shave, too. Things Vieve could not help him with at all and that would absolutely not be solved through the application of liver. Although she did assume a small, sparse fake mustache and a supercilious expression.

Pillover started to see bits of his father in the mirror when he wasn't expecting it as his cheeks thinned out. All these things contributed to the other boys teasing him even more than normal. He was gawky and awkward now, as well as scholarly and gloomy.

He didn't realize what kind of effect it might have on the fairer sex until he had to go to that ball at Sophronia's house.

His sister made him do it. His sister who didn't notice that he was now taller than she, probably because he had a propensity to slouch.

"Hoy up, Pustule." Dimity greeted him in the usual manner when he arrived for transport to the event in question.

"Hoy up, Petulance," was his gloomy response as he climbed into the open cart in the rain. He wasn't certain how he'd gotten himself into this. He didn't even like his sister. Why did he allow her to drag him into these things?

He looked around. "Agatha's not with you?"

Dimity tilted her head, big eyes mocking him.

He realized he'd made a blunder. "I like Agatha." He

defended himself. "She doesn't cheep-cheep on and on, unlike some people I know." They were siblings, after all. It was required of him to go on the attack when put in a defensive position.

Dimity lowered her lashes slyly. "She's not attending the ball. I'll tender your regards, shall I, brother dear?"

Pillover backed off hurriedly. "No need to fuss."

Dimity sat next to him and bumped his shoulder. Then, showing unexpected kindness, she dropped the subject.

Sophronia joined them in the cart (well, it was *her* cart). She brought along Lord Felix Mersey, which Pillover thought excessively unnecessary, not to say grotesque. Felix was one of Pillover's sworn enemies. Not that Felix knew about it. Just that he was a revolting bully of a toffy nob, whom Pillover intensely disliked. Felix's unpleasantness was the direct result of being both rich and handsome, a combination that made a mockery of fate. Felix could also be charming when he put his mind to it. Apparently Sophronia put him in mind. It made Pillover's stomach churn. He very much wished to bury himself in a book, but it was raining too hard to read. It was particularly annoying because he had something important to tell Sophronia, yet through the course of the entire cart ride and the ensuing preparations for the ball, he was never able to get her alone. Felix was always there.

The whole debacle lived on in his memory because it was his first exposure to girls of the nondirigible type. Normal girls, not spies, who had an interest in such things as marriage and curling tongs. Well, marriage that was not for political gain and curling tongs that were not for assassination.

He remembered numerous pretty girls twittering and fluttering about when he entered a room. And he remembered the exact moment when he realized it was because of *him*. There was something about *him* that they liked, for some reason. Not because they were obligated to pay him attention because of his sister. They did not even know he *had* a sister.

He overheard one of them say to another, "Don't you want to pet his head and coddle him? Poor boy, he seems so moribund."

"Do you think he writes poetry like Lord Byron? He looks like he might be a poet."

"He looks like the kind of boy that Mama would very much object to," giggled another.

Pillover was startled to realize this was a *good* thing.

"Perhaps he has had his heart broken."

"Or perhaps he wants to have it broken."

"Oh, and you think you're just the girl for it, do you, Amaryllis?"

When Pillover finally did manage to get Sophronia alone, that caused him even more problems. Later on in his life, he was to look back on that ball and the year that followed as *the year of troublesome females*.

He had a message from Sidheag for Sophronia that explained her whereabouts and why she'd disappeared all of a sudden. It came via Vieve, because Vieve was like that. Pillover was delivering it because Vieve had pointed her fake mustache at him in just such a way as to make his life miserable if he didn't do what she wanted. Vieve was dangerous when armed with a fake mustache. (Or should that be *lipped* with a fake mustache?)

Apparently Sidheag's werewolf pack had been disgraced for planning to kill Queen Victoria. Sidheag had gone to London to try to sort things out. Pillover found it all rather dramatic and mostly uninteresting – a bunch of supernaturals he cared little for. Certainly, if modern society had taught him nothing else, it was that supernaturals were best avoided (rather like girls). But he liked history and he knew that these kinds of incidents shaped it. So he managed a private consultation in the gazebo with Sophronia, to tell her everything. Plus there was Vieve's mustache to consider.

Pillover hadn't considered appearances. After all, he'd never been considered much of a threat to feminine virtue before, as a small, glum child with a head full of Latin.

He might still feel like a small, glum child, and his head was still full of Latin, but in outward appearance he was no longer so innocent a creature. Sophronia's mother found them. Together. Compromised.

"Sophronia Angelina Temminnick, what are you doing alone in a gazebo *with a boy*?" she screeched.

Both of them were rather dumbfounded. Pillover looked at Sophronia in surprise. Did she count as an actual girl? He supposed she did. Sophronia seemed to be looking at him with the same kind of mystification.

Mrs Temminnick, however, had kittens. "Mr Plumleigh-Teignmott, this is too bad! I'm shocked. Shocked, I say! After we welcomed you into our home. I trust you will make an honest woman of my daughter?"

"Mother. Pillover is barely fourteen."

Pillover frowned. Then realized he'd had a birthday recently. Goodness, fourteen. Seemed very old, all of a sudden.

"You're using his *given* name?" Sophronia's mother was even more aghast. "What have they been teaching you at that finishing school? Meeting a gentleman. In a gazebo. Alone and unchaperoned!"

"Really, Mother! He is a *child*. Don't be ridiculous."

Pillover could have told Sophronia that defensiveness was never a good tactic with mothers.

Also, he found it somewhat insulting to be so entirely dismissed. "Thank you kindly, Sophronia."

Sophronia continued to defend herself, which her mother took entirely amiss.

Eventually, Mrs Temminnick declared she would look into Pillover's family and arrange a match if she found his lineage suitable. Mrs Temminnick had a large brood, and being of only middling income, a vested interest in marrying off her daughters as quickly as possible. Pillover understood perfectly. He also understood that, on paper and without the evil genius component, he would present a tempting prospect – his parents were landed and he the only heir.

At the time, he'd exchanged looks with Sophronia, silently agreeing that there was no point in arguing further.

Which was how Pillover found himself sort of engaged to his sister's best friend. It was the first and only engagement of his life. He might have appreciated it more at the time if he'd known.

Sophronia said she would find a polite way to jilt him. She also started to call him a *lady-killer* because he cut such a swath at the ball. Pillover was not amused.

He tried not to cut swaths of any kind, but apparently the more reluctant he was and the more gloomy he appeared, the more the young ladies thought of him as some sort of tortured heroic figure ripe for swath-cutting. They had been reading far too much Brontë. Which he said to Vieve when he got back to Bunson's.

"Which Brontë?" wondered Vieve.

"Does it make a difference?" Pillover replied.

"Probably not." Vieve reached up, bracketed his face with two tiny hands, and then dragged him down for close examination. "I suppose I can somewhat see what the ladies are on about. If you like the type."

"I'm a *type* now?" objected Pillover.

Vieve nodded. "Face it. Silly girls like dyspeptic boys. They want to soothe your brow, dab your wounds, and cradle your emaciated form while you slowly die of consumption. You're morose, but it comes off as *sensitive*. Perhaps you should try to be more cheerful."

Pillover stared at his small friend, aghast. "Absolutely not. Don't be disgusting."

"Then you must face up to the fact that you are, indeed, a lady-killer."

Pillover curled his lip. "This is a tragedy. Possibly the great tragedy of my life."

"Yes, I believe that is the basis of the appeal."

Pillover was never entirely comfortable with the effect that he had on women and he was always grateful that Agatha seemed entirely immune. But Agatha was not the kind of girl who wished to sponge anyone's brow or dab at anyone's wound, except perhaps her own.

CHAPTER THREE
EXPLOSIVE DÉCOLLETAGE

December 1853 ~ Mademoiselle Geraldine's Finishing Academy for Young Ladies of Quality, somewhere over Devon

"You're engaged? To Sophronia?" Agatha had taken months to determine exactly how she was going to ask Pillover this question. She had practiced keeping her voice calm and her tone mild and disinterested. Still, it was hard to repress the quiver when he was right there in front of her. It hurt. At some point, and she wasn't certain when exactly, Agatha had begun to think of Pillover as a little bit hers. Belonging to himself first, of course, and to Dimity because he was her brother, but also to her.

Agatha wasn't wrong in that, was she? He always sought her out. The way he had that very night. He'd spotted her in her corner and made a beeline over. There had to be something significant about that. Something special in his noticing when no one else did. Didn't there?

Yet now he was engaged to her friend.

Sophronia talked about it as though it were all some great lark.

Agatha wanted Pillover's perspective.

He shuffled his feet and stared down at them, clearly uncomfortable with the subject of engagements in general and his in particular.

"What a clod rumpus," was his profound take. "Her mama, you understand? My goodness. I mean to say. Mothers. Belters. I say! What?"

Pillover was not a very eloquent boy. He was also giving her a very funny look. "Why so many sparkles tonight, Miss Woosmoss? You look as if you allowed my sister to decorate you."

Which, of course, she had. Agatha's assignment was to pretend to be Dimity this evening. To act like her friend and experience the ball as someone else. To perform as another person as part of her spycraft. To see how a more charming individual might extract information at a ball. Accordingly, she had dressed the part – or been dressed – but at the moment she wasn't bothering to *be* the part. Not with Dimity's brother. That seemed... unacceptably incestuous.

She looked up at him. He'd grown a great deal taller since the last time she'd seen him. He'd also unwittingly assumed the mannerisms of an idle reprobate – a slouching, sneering disinterest in social structures and a propensity to look away during conversation as though his soul were focused on deeper matters. In actuality, he was probably declining Latin nouns in his head. But to Agatha's intense annoyance, other ladies, even trained ones, found this new version of Pillover appealing. No doubt this was a result of his mannerisms, not his nouns. She knew that one of the reasons Pillover had sought her out was to avoid an excess of feminine attention.

"Good evening, Mr Plumleigh-Teignmott," she said,

moving to leave her corner, somewhat annoyed at the whole situation.

He caught her arm.

"Crikey, Miss Woosmoss, I meant no offense. I did just compare you to my sister. That must be distressing. I do apologize. I shall say no more on the subject. Although," he looked furtively around, "you have been gaining in the social game. That gown is topping."

Agatha acknowledged this fact and also hated it. Hated that even Pillover had noticed. Pillover, who barely noticed *anything*. Agatha was playing the game because it was required of her, but Dimity had stuffed her into a dress that was rather too tight, especially on the top. As a result, it put significant parts of her anatomy on display by virtue of the fact that she had been cursed with a great deal more of said parts than Dimity. Agatha, as a result, had been *noticed* by several of the young gentlemen in attendance and she did not like it.

Now even Pillover, notorious in his dismissal of fashion, had been moved to comment. Although from his frown, he too did not like it, for all that his words had flattered.

"It has pink ruffles," said Agatha morosely.

Pillover nodded. Gloomy was his preferred state and he sank quickly back into it with her. Now that they could mutually complain about something, all their earlier awkwardness was forgotten. "They must be very trying for you."

"And I am laced so tightly I can barely breathe."

"Whatever for?"

"To fit into the ruffles."

"Pernicious ruffles. I always thought there was something innately suspicious about them."

"It's fluttering purgatory," agreed Agatha.

"Not too different from being engaged to Sophronia," said Pillover.

"That bad, is it?"

"Perfectly ghastly." He brightened a bit. "Although I did just talk to her and she said she would be throwing me over in the not too distant future. So there is some hope."

They stood, propping up the wall, and watched everyone else be effortlessly effervescent for a while.

Pillover gave her an uncertain look. "Should we dance, do you think?"

Agatha sighed. "It is a ball, and I am supposed to be pretending to be your sister."

"Are you indeed? Well, that makes it somewhat odd, doesn't it? Should you be dancing with me under those circumstances?"

"Ah, I should say I'm supposed to be pretending to be your sister's breed of personality."

"You're not doing a particularly brilliant job."

"No, I'm not. I was trying, but now I'm hiding."

"My sister would, however, dance if asked," Pillover said, almost timidly. "Cannot I help you a little with your pretense? It might be easier to flirt with me, whom you know, than any of these other blighters." He gestured at the conceited mass of Bunson's boys in a highly disgusted manner.

Agatha suspected he was right. Plus she really should pretend to do as she'd been instructed. She wasn't sure it was smart, flirting with Pillover, but if he already knew it was all an act, then it couldn't be too bad, could it?

So she allowed him to lead her out on the dance floor and into a waltz.

Agatha pretended liveliness and adoration and Pillover, at first quite uncomfortable with her attention, eventually grew into a tacit acceptance. His own expression remained glum, but there was a certain twinkle to his eye that suggested he was game to play his part to the best of his meager abilities. Which, admittedly, were paltry. Pillover would never be able to tread the boards.

"Of what do we talk?" he asked while they twirled sedately around the floor. "A young man in my position ought to brag, don't you think? Of his achievements, I mean."

"If he has any. It's either that or recite poetry."

Pillover wrinkled his nose. "I have some Latin verse memorized, if you would prefer?"

"Oh no, please, brag away. Do."

Pillover was a passable dancer. Apparently evil geniuses were required to have the basics by rote. Agatha waited patiently while he considered his options.

"Oh, right, yes! I have attained Nefarious Genius ranking. That's something *like*, is it not?"

Agatha pretended to be very impressed and fluttered her lashes up at him. "You don't say? But I thought you didn't want to actually become a full Evil Genius. And here you have *progressed*."

"Oh, I don't want it. But Vieve has helped me to develop this augmentation for devices. Now most everything I make explodes upon contact. I don't really have to worry about the device itself functioning for its intended purpose anymore. All I have to do is make sure it blows up when anyone picks it up. The professors are very impressed and bang's your biscuit, everyone thinks I'm admirably terrible. It's masterly. The Pistons have mostly stopped pestering me. Lord Dingleproops nearly lost an eyebrow to my hair tonic applicator only last week. I was cursed. He cursed *me*. Best day of my life."

"Well done, you!" said Agatha. Pillover was rather getting into the spirit of waltzing and bragging, and she liked it when he opened up and just *talked* to her. He did it as though nothing else really mattered, as though he just wanted to chat. It was nice. Honest. There wasn't a great deal of honesty in Agatha's life. It was unaffected and adorable.

"Thank you. It's made it much easier to spend most of my time studying history and dead languages and suchlike. Not the education my parents would have wished for me, of course. And I must remember not to touch the explosive devices myself, but all in all, a satisfactory outcome."

Agatha winced in concern. "Do be careful. The last thing you need is to lose a finger or some other appendage in a spate of absentmindedness."

Pillover nodded. "Too true. Very embarrassing. Now, what shall we talk about next?"

"The weather?" suggested Agatha.

"No, I don't think that works. Shouldn't you be trying to extract information from me or some such rot?"

"I could do that with the weather."

"Could you, indeed? Well, then. Carry on."

So they talked of the weather. Agatha learned that Pillover liked the rain, when it was outside and he did not have to be in it, of course. "It makes me feel cozy and pleased to be reading and not as if there were a whole wide world out there overwhelming me with possibilities that I do not like."

Agatha nodded. "I don't like rain," she admitted, in a rare moment of confession. But this was only Pillover – nobody minded if he actually knew something real about her. "I like warm weather and the sun."

"Hardly likely to find much of that here in jolly old England."

"Which is why I want to travel."

"Do you really? How extraordinary."

"Don't you?" Agatha cocked her head, genuinely surprised. She thought it was a sentiment most people at least verbalized, even if they didn't really feel it. It was true for her, though. For as long as she could remember she'd dreamed of foreign lands and exotic places. She could not recall a time when she'd wished to stay in England.

"Absolutely not. Travel seems a highly incommodious business. All that larking about. I suppose the desire does suit your line of work." Pillover was alluding to her intelligencer future. It was pleasant to talk to someone who simply assumed that was what she would be doing with her life. Agatha's friends did not believe that she would actually graduate from finishing school. Of course, she was deluding them into that belief. But Pillover did not care what his sister might have said about how bad Agatha was at her lessons. He only knew that she had never told him otherwise. He had said to her that he did not want to be an Evil Genius and assumed that if she did not want to be a spy, she would have been similarly forthcoming. Pillover did not judge, he accepted until informed otherwise.

"Where do you want to go?" he asked.

Agatha realized that somehow she'd allowed him to distract her and was in danger of failing her current mission. Both the fake one, where she was using Dimity's personality to extract information, and the real one, where she was supposed to be gleaning information to send to Lord Akeldama. Pillover was of little help on that front. She must dance with other, more evil and well connected boys.

"Everywhere," she said, elusively.

"Wales?" suggested Pillover.

"I was thinking rather further afield."

Pillover nodded, somber. "Seems dangerous."

"Yes, but sunny."

"Fair point. Ah, speaking of which, I have a small gift

for you. Might it be a good thing to give it publicly, so your professors can witness it?" The waltz having ended, he escorted her off the dance floor.

Agatha nodded.

Pillover pressed a small, wrapped object into her hand.

"It won't explode, will it?"

Pillover's serious face was made striking and unfairly beautiful by a sudden smile. "No, it's only a Depraved Lens of Crispy Magnification, but it could be very useful in places where there is sun."

Agatha faked a laugh and tucked the gift down her cleavage, because it was right there on display and it was something that might definitely attract the attention of the wrong sort of useful boy.

Pillover's eyes bugged. Agatha felt a little embarrassed. She hadn't thought he'd be affected. He looked faint.

"Was that necessary?" he squeaked.

"Hush, you. I believe my dance card is about to be full."

Pillover snatched the carte de bal away from her and filled in a later set.

Agatha whipped out a fan. "A *second* waltz, Mr Plumleigh-Teignmott? Surly you ask too much."

"You're getting rather too good at this, Miss Woosmoss," said Pillover, bowing and making himself scarce.

Agatha was popular at the ball after that. Although she tried hard not to be *too* popular. She wanted to pass the test, but not with flying colors. Later she would blame Dimity's pink ruffles for all her success. And she would try never again to be the center of attention like that. But she would also admit, late at night in a private missive to Lord Akeldama for she had no other confessor, to liking the attention just a little bit.

She did not tell the vampire that her liking had included Pillover's startled face. And the way he flushed slightly. The way he swallowed audibly when he danced with her a second time. Her own feminine wiles, as it turned out, were a heady kind of power. It was a remarkable thing to hold sway over a man, any man, even Pillover. Especially Pillover.

Sophronia thanked her later because Pillover's marked public preference for Agatha had afforded her the perfect opportunity to cry off their engagement. Agatha was pleased with that result, too, although she did not let that show to anyone.

She treasured her magnification lens. It was the first gift a boy had ever given her, and it was a useful one. She used it for years, in many sunny places and foreign lands. More than once it extracted her from a very sticky situation. And it did not explode.

~

New Year's Eve 1853 ~ Mademoiselle Geraldine's Finishing Academy for Young Ladies of Quality, somewhere over Devon

Decades could pass, but no matter how forgetful he became, Pillover would never forget the time his sister's finishing school crashed out of the sky. It was to be the end of Agatha's education (his sister's and Sophronia's too). For obvious reasons, one could not go back and pursue higher learning in a dirigible that no longer floated at all high. Pillover remembered it not only because it was the ending of a great many more things than just Mademoiselle Geraldine's, but also because he had the dubious pleasure of experiencing the entire event live and in person.

Mostly he remembered how frightened he was. And how not frightened his sister and her friends were. All the ladies behaved so very capably in that crisis while Pillover and the other gentlemen present acquitted themselves like panicked quail crossing a frozen puddle. It was a lesson he never forgot. It was to lead him into a lifelong admiration for capable women and an equally lifelong suspicion of puddles.

The New Year's tea party was in full vibration when Pillover joined it. What had probably started as mild talk and meek encounters around set tables had descended into a proper rout. The young persons were circulating freely, seeking preferred partners or more engaging conversation. There was even some questionable dancing. Pillover could guess from their purposeful expressions that a few of the young ladies had assignments. He'd had a long enough association with the school to at least spot intent, even if he could not identify specifics. That was by design, of course. He was only an evil genius in training. He had no particular interest in countering intelligencers in action, let alone young ladies of quality enjoying themselves at play. He was rarely a target and he planned to engage in a life of obscurity well away from politics or performances, so it hardly mattered that he could spot them in action. He never intended to reveal to anyone that he could, regardless.

What he noticed that worried him was not the lady spies. No, it was the fact that while there were many familiar faces amongst the Bunson's boys in attendance, somehow at some point, strangers had come aboard. And not strangers who were other Bunson's students to whom Pillover had not yet been properly introduced. These were *actual* strangers – boys whom Pillover had never seen before in his life. Some of them were even adult men pretending to be boys. It was highly unsettling. Pillover knew he must tell Agatha about it. Because Agatha would know what to do.

So Pillover began frantically circling the tea party looking for one telltale redhead. But Agatha had only become better over the years at disappearing during social gatherings. Except for that one time when she'd been pretending to be Dimity, she remained invisible. Pillover had trained his eye as best he could to spot her, but an amateur like himself could no longer go up against a professional like Agatha.

Pillover could not spot Agatha anywhere at that tea party.

He thought to get hold of his sister or Sophronia, but both of them had joined the group of mixed couples dancing – if such a spectacle might be dignified with the term. Perhaps *cavorting* was a better moniker. Pillover was not made of stern enough stuff to cut in on Sophronia mid-cavort. One simply did not cut in on a lady of her character. He might be interrupting something deadly. And at his age, it would be too humiliating to be seen to dance with his sister at all, let alone risk a cut in order to do so. He shuddered to think. No, he had to find Agatha.

Pillover did get briefly distracted by the food on offer. The tea was mighty fine, and there was champagne as well, a thing never once to grace the halls of Bunson's. Geraldine's girls must learn everything, including how to apply, manipulate, and, when occasion demanded, imbibe alcohol – for queen and country! Pillover paused in his Agatha hunt to stash a Scotch seedcake in his waistcoat pocket and look longingly at the glazed apples before having to acknowledge the fact that any attempt to pilfer would result in irreparable damage to his attire. He then stuffed his face with orange biscuits dipped in medlar jelly, because who wouldn't? He seriously considered a wedge of almond torte, but almond was too near to cyanide for his peace of mind, so he gave it a pass.

Then, he spotted Agatha. His mistake had been to assume she was wallflowering on the periphery of the room. She was, in fact, at a table in the middle, seated with an abandoned tea service in front of her, having somehow become part of the furniture. Pillover supposed it made sense that when there was so much activity at a gathering, to stand still on the outskirts was more obvious than to sit hunched in the center.

He made his way over and slumped into the chair next to her. "Top of the evening to you, Miss Woosmoss."

"Mr Plumleigh-Teignmott. How did you notice me?" She sounded tired and a little annoyed. She looked wan, as though this was all a terrible trial to her nerves. He perfectly understood – such a noisy gathering of his peers in ecstasies was a trial to his finer feelings. It was all very well and good to be happy, but did they have to be so obvious about it?

"It did take a me a while. I searched the perimeter first."

"I suppose it makes a difference that you know to look for me and do so intentionally."

"Of course it does." Pillover was affronted on Agatha's behalf. "Plus there's the red hair to consider. Although I will say it has become harder over the years to spot you, even though the shade of your hair remains unchanged. There will likely come a time when even I cannot find you at a party, no matter how much I might desire it."

"Nevertheless, the fact that you *want* to find me makes all the difference. Most don't and so it is easy for them not to. The nature of intent is key. People often will not see what they do not want to."

"You do enjoy being overlooked." Pillover plucked at a discarded scone.

"Do I?"

"Oh. You don't take pleasure in it? I would."

Agatha cracked a smile at that. "What can I do for you, Mr Plumleigh-Teignmott?"

"I regret to inform you that there are strangers amongst my classmates. I think your school is being infiltrated." Pillover got straight to the point. He couldn't abide shilly-shallying.

"What kind of strangers?"

"I don't know. All I know is that they are non-Bunson ones. Aren't the particulars your responsibility?"

Agatha tilted her head. "You might have become an intelligencer yourself, if you had liked it well enough. Did you know?"

Pillover was absolutely appalled at the idea. It was almost worse than being an evil genius.

"You *are* a keen observer," she pointed out.

"I am not!" Pillover was upset at the accusation.

Agatha flicked out her fan and hid a smile. "No insult intended. My apologies for having mentioned it. I shall not do so again."

"Quite right, see that you don't."

Agatha's attention shifted and she caught someone's eye across the room. She dropped her fan and pulled a fine silk handkerchief from her cleavage.

Pillover blushed and looked away. Agatha was endowed generously and he was having an increasingly difficult time not attending to this fact.

Fortunately, her odd behavior distracted him. She raised the handkerchief to her face and wiped it across her lips, although she had not recently eaten anything. Pillover followed her gaze, wondering if she were attempting to seduce someone, and not liking that idea at all. Plus who seduced via messy eating habits?

She was looking at Sophronia and Dimity, who had paused their gyratory dancing operations and were at the refreshment table, seemingly equally flummoxed by Agatha's odd behavior.

Pillover could see them talking to each other while they stared across the room. He gave them a flap of his hand in as close to a *come hither* gesture as he could manage, given his own personality. It probably looked more dismissive than welcoming. It didn't matter – they weren't looking at him, but still staring at Agatha.

Couples and small groups of girls scuttled between them.

"What are you doing?" he asked.

"Trying to get them to come over." Agatha wiped her lip again.

"Is that code?"

"Oh really, Pillover, it's normal ball behavior. Have you never learned any of the standard social niceties of flirtatious accessory communication? Fan? Handkerchief? Parasol?"

"Not so as I'd remember. What did you say?"

"I told them that I desired their acquaintance."

This did not make her handkerchief manipulation any less murky. "But aren't they your very dear friends already?"

Agatha rolled her eyes at him. "Yes, that's the point. I want them to come over here."

His sister was shaking her head at Agatha.

"See there," said Pillover, "Dimity doesn't know what you want, either. Shall we go to them?" He made to rise and offered his arm.

"I cannot cause a stir just at the moment. Sister Mattie is watching. Your sitting here with me is already unusual."

"Ah, should I make myself scarce, then?" Pillover didn't want to leave. They barely had any time to talk together anymore. He wanted to maximize what little time he had. But he understood that Agatha was at work, in her way. He hated to be disturbed when he was translating Latin verse. Surely this was not dissimilar. Besides, he had given her the information in the hopes that she might know what to do with it. His part in the game had been discharged.

"No. Please stay. Tell them what you know. They may have questions for you that I have not considered."

"You trivialize yourself," objected Pillover. He suspected that Agatha was much better at all of this than anyone knew, or gave her credit for.

"Hush now, dear. I'm busy."

Pillover slouched back, pleased and delighted both to stay and to have been called *dear*, even if it was Agatha's version of a joke.

Agatha raised her free hand and wound the handkerchief around her third finger.

"What did you say this time?" he asked.

"I am married."

Pillover arched a brow. He realized at that moment that if Agatha Woosmoss were to marry anyone, it should be him. Also that this meant he had a great deal of growing up to do.

"I say, that's not sporting. Hardly gave me a chance." He made a joke of it, because he thought that was the best tactic, and at least she might get a hint of his intent.

It worked, because she giggled at him. Actually giggled. "You're an infant. And I'm trying to confuse them enough to come over here out of frustration, if nothing else."

The *infant* comment stung.

Across the room, Sophronia was shaking her head at Agatha. Pillover sensed this was from annoyance more than anything.

Agatha gave a theatrical sigh, which drew Pillover's

eyes back to *that* part of her anatomy and made him come over hot and self-conscious.

"Why are they being so stubborn?" she asked, as if he had insight into his sister's character (let alone Sophronia's).

Pillover tugged the handkerchief away from Agatha and began gesticulating with it himself. If Agatha wanted them confused, he could certainly help with that. He flicked it out, once, then scrunched it into a ball and dropped it to the table.

Agatha shook her head and grabbed it back.

"What did I say?" Pillover wanted to know.

"You told them you were a new bride."

Pillover laughed. "That'll teach me not to waggle handkerchiefs in languages I do not speak. Come on, then, let's just risk it and go over to them. We're wasting time with this nonsense."

Agatha tucked the handkerchief away. Pillover envied the bit of silk its accommodations, and then led her in a circuitous route over to his sister and her friend.

They had to cross the part of the room being used for dancing. Feeling daring, Pillover swept Agatha up into his arms in what he hoped was a manly way, and swirled her around, imitating the other couples until the set brought them close to Dimity and Sophronia.

∽

Agatha, watching the Tunstell twins bicker as they floated home to London, was reminded of Pillover and Dimity. She remembered that time at the New Year's Eve ball when Pillover had insisted upon verbally sparring with his sister by way of greeting despite the urgency of the situation. Apparently sibling social relationships demanded that all conversation open with insult even at the expense of vital information.

It had been up to Agatha to get them into the meat of the matter. "There are strangers hidden amongst the boys attending our festivities. Strangers to Bunson's, I mean."

Sophronia and Dimity glanced about the room, eyes drawn to the various gentlemen present.

"Yes indeed. Picklemen and their associates, I suspect." Sophronia did not seem at all surprised. Picklemen were a long-running foe of hers. Agatha knew that her friend kept close track of them, and could identify them even when they were disguised as schoolboys. Sophronia was like that about secret societies, which is to say, wary and careful with them.

Agatha was a little disappointed that she and Pillover had not provided new information. Pillover looked crestfallen. He did so like being helpful, even if the end result was not to his taste. It was awfully endearing.

"As secret societies go, they are one of the very worst," said Dimity. "I should prefer not to fraternize with them."

Agatha thought that rather underplayed the situation and hid a smile.

"Secret societies are, on the whole, deeply inconvenient," agreed Pillover. "They always have *agendas*."

Agatha thought that agendas were inherently problematic for someone like Pillover, who had none of his own and no interest in promoting anyone else's. Because people with agendas could never understand the Pillovers of the world.

Dimity tutted at her brother. "You simply hate participating in *anything*."

"It's dashed inconvenient, that's what. Secret societies always involve meetings and coded greetings. They make everything unnecessarily complicated. Life is quite complicated enough without *planning* agendas. Don't you go joining any secret societies, sister. I shall never forgive you!"

Agatha looked at Sophronia, curious. "How did you know?" She shook her head. "I genuinely thought that Pillover had put me at an advantage, for once."

Sophronia didn't explain, not that Agatha had expected her to. Sophronia had always been good about safeguarding her methods. Instead, she asked Pillover to point out the exact infiltrators. Unfortunately, they all seemed to have vanished.

"Scarpered." Pillover shook his head, looking despondent.

"You're useless," said his sister.

"Did I say I wished to be useful?" Pillover shot back.

Agatha was made uncomfortable by Pillover's genuine hurt and Dimity's sisterly disregard. Sometimes Dimity could be unknowingly cruel to her little brother. Weirdly, she felt protective. After all, he'd come to her with the information and now was being shamed for trying to help. Agatha frowned. Well, if Sophronia had known all along, Agatha could rest assured that she would solve for the ultimate equation, and all she need do was watch and take mental notes to report back to Lord Akeldama later.

So she turned to Pillover and offered her card, using his disappointment and confusion to elicit a dance. She knew he did not enjoy dancing, and frankly neither did she, but she did like being held in his arms, and dancing was really her only option for that particular activity. He did seem to cheer up a little in her company.

Of course, Agatha had made a miscalculation.

She had trusted a little too highly in Sophronia's abilities. Even Sophronia, as it turned out, could not stop what those infiltrators had started. Because they were intelligencers, they had all miscalculated. Sophronia, like Agatha, had assumed that the infiltrators were there to learn and manipulate. When, it transpired that, they were there to sabotage – lacking all style or finesse.

In this particular instance, what they did caused the dirigible to fall out of the sky. Something not even Sophronia could stop from happening.

This inevitability was heralded by a low booming noise that reverberated through the party, causing the whole room to shudder.

CHAPTER FOUR

HOW NOT TO CRASH A DIRIGIBLE

New Year's Eve 1853 ~ Mademoiselle Geraldine's Finishing Academy for Young Ladies of Quality, somewhere over (and rather quickly in) Devon

Pillover did not like the sensation of the dirigible he was inside of shivering like a wet puppy. He had no fear of heights, but now had the sinking suspicion he was about to develop one. Emphasis on the term *sinking*.

Around him students screamed, mostly the gentlemen, but a few of the ladies as well. Several groups made for the door in clusters of silken skirts and decorative waistcoats. The gentlemen hunted for their top hats (as if hats would help when one was inside a misbehaving dirigible).

At a loss for what else to do, Pillover searched out Agatha. After their dance she'd given him the slip, but she was easy to spot for a change, as she was standing with Dimity and Sophronia.

The airship began to list to one side, the floor of the

room becoming alarmingly tilted. Pillover skidded over to the girls, trying to calculate the angle of repose.

"One of the balloons must be down," Agatha explained to him consolingly when he chivvied up. This did not inspire a great deal of confidence. When she gave him a tentative smile, he was even more unsettled. Agatha's smiles meant nerves, not pleasure.

"Not to worry," said Sophronia, "We have two other balloons."

"Since we remain excessively tilted, you'll forgive me for worrying," replied Pillover, who thought he would soon be moving past worry into the emotional jungle of outright panic. "One out of three balloons is still a third less support than we had mere moments ago."

"Oh, you and your mathematics!" complained Dimity.

There came another massive booming noise, which this time was followed by an abrasive clanging bell. The dirigible continued to shudder and list.

Pillover suspected that might be a second balloon gone. Mathematics were now actively working against them. He pointed a trembling finger at Sophronia, because he suspected her of being involved. She always seemed to be involved in disasters. "I loathe adventure. Have I mentioned that recently? This is your fault, is it not? You've arranged an entirely unwarranted adventure for us all, haven't you? Ruddy uncalled for, if you ask me."

Sophronia frowned. "I don't believe so. Not this time. Sorry, Pill, you can't blame me for this one."

That made matters worse, because if it wasn't Sophronia it meant she didn't have a plan to get them out of it. And much as he disliked an agenda, at least Sophronia's agendas were usually successful.

Dimity ignored him and looked at her friend. "I do

believe that we are under attack. That would explain the embarrassingly loud booms. And the proximity alarms."

Pillover jumped at the sensation of a gentle hand on his arm. Agatha was patting him softly. It was very nice of her, but he wished she'd chosen to touch him at a point in time when his heart wasn't beating out of his chest and his entire body sheened in a cold sweat. He definitely could not properly appreciate the sensation of her affection.

The whole school shook violently again.

Pillover's stomach churned. He thought he might faint and regretted every bit of cake he'd eaten that evening.

"Do you think this is the work of the Picklemen or the flywaymen?" asked Agatha, unfortunately removing her hand from his arm.

"Maybe both." Sophronia's tone was dark. She was looking around the room. "Where, oh where do you suppose all our pretty Pistons have gone?"

Pillover looked around, too, noticing what she had. That not only had all the mysterious infiltrating strangers disappeared, but so had all the Pistons. The scourge of his first few years at Bunson's. The bad boys with rich parents and too much status, who had too many gears on their outfits and too much time on their hands – they had all vanished. Mersey and Dingleproops and their cadre of layabouts were all gone.

Dimity, being his sister and a silly bint, misconstrued Sophronia's statement. "You cannot possibly be thinking of flirting now."

Sophronia shook her head at Dimity's silliness. "Certainly not. I am, in fact, thinking about taking cover. I believe we may be falling out of the sky."

"Well, isn't that splendid?" said Pillover, hoping she was finally taking action, and that he could follow.

The floor of the room was now tilted so severely that it

was nigh impossible for Pillover to remain upright without leaning excessively to counteract. He must look ridiculous, sickly-faced and angled like a tree grown in stiff breezes. Around them, tables and chairs and people had mostly slid toward one wall.

The entire event was occurring quite slowly and sedately. The act of floating was always considered the most dignified mode of travel – apparently even a dirigible crash was dignified.

"Oh, dear me, yes, we do appear to be sinking," said his sister, finally understanding the gravity of the situation.

"Come along, then." Sophronia led them on a kind of half slip, half slide downhill and up against the wall with all the furniture. "The airship is going down. Brace yourselves."

"How can you be so certain?" Pillover asked, because he lived in hope.

Sophronia pointed with her chin to where the missing Pistons had flipped a large table on its edge, and were perched behind it like soldiers at a barricade. If the ship continued to list, they would be effectively protected from flying furniture, comestibles, and young ladies of quality. Pillover was ashamed to see they had invited neither ladies nor comestibles to join them. Did they not care for the finer things in life? How very ungentlemanly.

The floor was now at a forty-five-degree angle. Pillover was haunted by the mathematics of it all. He could not stop calculating. He thought about statistical odds on surviving a dirigible collapse. Hadn't he read a scientific paper on the number of airship accidents reported to the Home Office last year?

All around him, young ladies and gentlemen were losing their battles with gravity and going tumbling themselves. Fluffy petticoats and even more unmentionable underthings were being put on full display. Anywhere Pillover looked he could see things he was tolerably certain no innocent young man of his age ought to see. There were *ankles*, for goodness sake. A few unfortunate ladies were showing whole legs with stockings *and* drawers. Pillover did the only thing he could do under such trying circumstances – he fainted.

So it was that Pillover Plumleigh-Teignmott was indeed there at the historic moment when Mademoiselle Geraldine's Finishing Academy for Young Ladies of Quality crashed into Dartmoor. He was, in fact, on board. But he did not actually experience it, because he was insensible. He would remember only what happened before and what happened after.

He was never certain whether he ought to be grateful for this or not.

But the next thing he recalled was Agatha waking him up with a not gentle slap to the cheek. And then a long, dark, cold walk over wet grass, through heather and gorse, in shoes meant for dancing, not trooping the wild moors. A bleak, dim memory, shattered by what came next – Agatha and her confession. For Pillover was to witness how far his sister's friendships might extend when fractured by betrayal.

∼

New Year's Eve 1853 ~ Dartmoor

Agatha remembered being scared when the school dirigible fell from the sky, but not as scared as she probably should have been. It did not, for example, instill in her a lifelong fear of floating. If anything, she floated almost as much now as she had then, and back then she'd *lived* aboard an airship.

Now she just used them to get around all the time. Now dirigibles went further and faster because the aetherosphere had been charted and the technology vastly improved. Now there were days, sometimes weeks, she spent in the grey – like right now, which reminded her more than anything else of her youth aboard a floating finishing school in the soft mists of Dartmoor. Probably why she was thinking about it now. Oddly, she remembered little of the fall itself.

Afterwards, they'd tromped through the wet grasses of the moor for a while before Sophronia became agitated and adamant that she must return to the dirigible alone. That she had to defend it against whoever had sunk it. That there was something important about the school itself that made the evacuation dangerous, not to those who had been evacuated, but to the world if the school was left unprotected. And because it was Sophronia, everyone believed her.

"You can't come with me," she'd said. "There are things you must do groundside. Someone has to ride to London and report the flywaymen to the authorities. It can't be Pillover. He hasn't the training, not to mention his general reticence."

Pillover looked like he might protest, but Agatha could tell he was mostly just relieved not to be asked. She could see where Sophronia was going with this. Dimity would stay behind to protect evacuated students and staff, and she, Agatha, would go to London.

Sophronia continued, explaining what Agatha had already deduced. "The Dewan must come here to help Soap. He is his Alpha, after all. Plus, as the queen's representative, he has to know that the school was attacked. Although how to actually get a message to him once in London is a problem."

Agatha knew her time had come. She had always suspected it would be sooner rather than later. She'd always intended to tell them once they graduated, anyway, but this seemed like a more significant moment. Now, with the school down, and the teachers and students marching across the moor, she had a feeling that things were ending. It was time for her to reveal her secrets and take the hits as they might fall. Now, when the connections she had in London would be of greatest use.

So Agatha did something she had never done before – she interrupted Sophronia. She let her voice be sharp and confident. "I can get a message to the Dewan." And she could, easily. Because she knew Lord Akeldama, and in London, Lord Akeldama could get to *anyone*, even the queen.

Sophronia was wearing a most gratifying stupefied expression. "*You*, Agatha?"

Agatha took one last long look at the faces of her friends. At Sophronia, proud, sharp-eyed and angular. At Dimity, softly sweet and persuasive. At Pillover, sullen and dyspeptic. They looked at her with love. Yes, even Pillover. And she was about to break that open and see how deep that love went and whether it was coupled with understanding and, if possible, forgiveness.

"You never guessed, did you?" Agatha said to her friends. Her real friends of four years whom she now risked losing. A decision she had made before the idea of friends was even a possibility might now cost her all of them. It was time to expose what she'd done behind their backs all along.

Sophronia's eyes went hard, the moonlight making harsh planes of her cheeks. "Guessed what, Agatha?"

Dimity had a hand over her mouth, prepared to perform the appropriate shock for no one's benefit but her own.

Agatha drew herself up and took a breath, a little winded by the long walk, truth be told.

Pillover was staring at her in a fixed manner. His eyes

moved from her face to her chest when she inhaled. This boy liked her figure and was too young to hide that fact. Agatha liked him for it. Liked how genuine he always was with her. Liked that there was one person in her life without artifice. And now she was going to ruin that, too.

"All along, I've been working for someone else."

"You mean the entire time we've been at school together, you've had a patron?" Sophronia liked people to be precise with their information.

Agatha nodded. "Truth be told, my papa is not all *that* rich."

Dimity squealed. "Oh, Agatha, how could you?"

Sophronia's brow wrinkled. She wasn't happy about this but, if Agatha read her face and her character correctly, once Sophronia got over her shock, she would be impressed. "All along? For four years? Were you assigned to infiltrate the school from the start or were you sent here for training?"

Agatha tilted her head. "Both, actually."

Despite herself, Agatha found her gaze drawn to Pillover. To her delight, he didn't seem upset. He didn't even seem shocked. If anything, his normal gloom had lightened to approval.

"You don't seem at all surprised, Mr Plumleigh-Teignmott." Had she underestimated him, or did Pillover just not care for her as much as she hoped?

Pillover shrugged in that annoying way of his. "I always figured you were special," he explained. "It's the lack of chatter, you see?"

Dimity, unlike her brother, was on the edge of tears. "Oh, Agatha, how could you? You aren't..." She trailed off, gave a whimper. "You aren't working for *them*, are you?"

"Them who?" Agatha suppressed a wince, feeling a sympathetic welling in her own eyes. She hadn't wanted to hurt her friend this much. She hadn't realized that she could.

"The flywaymen?" Dimity whispered.

"No."

"The Picklemen?" Dimity's voice was a touch more confident. Hopeful.

"Absolutely not."

"The Westminster Hive? Alongside Monique?"

"Not exactly," Agatha hedged, not wanting to lie anymore.

"Lord Akeldama." Of course Sophronia would figure it out. She understood the machinations of London politics, and she liked to keep track of the movers and shakers in the supernatural set.

Agatha felt her face go still and her skin prickle into goose bumps down her arms. She nodded firmly.

Sophronia grinned at her. Big and wide and genuine. "Very nicely done, Agatha. Are you set up to become one of his drones, once all this is finished?"

Agatha was so relieved she almost stumbled from it. She found herself clutching her bosom with one hand because of the pounding underneath. As if she were in some staged melodrama.

She tightened her lips to prevent her own grin. "Lord Akeldama doesn't take females, as a rule. Although he once offered for you in a carriage about town." By which statement she was offering evidence of her abilities, her intimacies, and her contacts.

Sophronia had never told Agatha about the private drive when Lord Akeldama tried to recruit her. But Lord Akeldama had told Agatha about it. She'd been under orders to befriend Sophronia from the very beginning. She liked to think she would have done it anyway, but the fact remained that everything had started as an assignment for her. What friendships were strong enough to survive such a beginning?

Agatha felt that she owed them an explanation. She looked at her own pudgy hands. There was a freckle on her pinky finger that no amount of lemon juice could remove. Her face in the mirror was pudgy and freckled, too. How to explain to Sophronia and Dimity, who were both so beautiful? "You are so pretty, Sophronia. It makes everything easier. Who wants you. What you can do. Whom you can work for. You'll be able to work as an intelligencer forever. For as long as you want. Because you are also good at it."

Sophronia looked as though she was going to interrupt, so Agatha pressed on. "I am dowdy and invisible. I am the ultimate wallflower."

Dimity made a noise of sad protest. She always hated it when Agatha talked down about herself. She didn't understand what Agatha was trying to explain. Even Pillover looked concerned.

Frustrated, Agatha said, "No. Please don't concern yourself with my finer feelings. I assure you I understand what I am good at. But I also understand that I am, most of the time, an object of pity. What you don't see is that's useful, too. It doesn't make a girl feel all that nice most of the time. But he saw through it, you understand? From the very first time we met. I was so young, but he saw me. *He* did. When no one else ever did, not even my own blood. He won't take me for a drone and he won't put me in the field where my talents aren't up to Sophronia's standards."

Agatha aimed to fix that part. It was going to take time, but she thought she could do it. Prove it to the vampire. Lord Akeldama was ancient and immortal and powerful, but he was also open to manipulation, especially from someone like Agatha. Beautiful people always underestimated those who were not. The vampire was smart enough to recognize Agatha's abilities for what they were – the polar opposite of his own – but that made him vulnerable. He couldn't predict her because he didn't understand her. Any man who had lived as long as Lord Akeldama had was capable of changing his mind, which meant Agatha could change it for him.

"So if he's not going to turn you into a drone or use you as an intelligencer, what are you getting out of this arrangement?"

Agatha lowered her gaze, looked again at her hands, now clenched. "Enough money to set up my own household, if I want." She did not look at Pillover as she lied. She didn't want to see hope in his face. But she could not tell the truth, because her friends wouldn't understand. Especially not Dimity. They, all of them, wanted to fit in, to find their places, to belong in some concrete way to this society. To London. To this tiny green island.

Agatha did not. She wanted to escape it all. But to explain to a guard dog why a wolf runs is fruitless. For the dog only knows that she must guard, and the wolf only knows that she must run.

"No!" Dimity gasped. She put a hand to her throat, a learned maneuver well executed, and now habit.

Pillover gave his sister a disgusted look.

Agatha continued. "I would be an independent woman of means. I could love as I willed without consulting my family. He even promised me an allowance, if I continued to pass on information." And she intended to prove her worth so much and so well that eventually there would come a time when the vampire needed to send her into Europe. Because there were always certain things a confirmed spinster of invisibility could do that a single man of style could not. Certain places only she could go. And after she proved her worth in France or Spain, then perhaps Prussia. And after that, India. And after that some faraway land where a language she had never learned would roll over her like waves of lost music and she could finally forget herself.

"So you can get a message to Lord Akeldama, and he'll alert the Dewan?" Sophronia, as ever, was not to be distracted by something so trivial as a friend's betrayal. She had an airship to save and a mission she had assigned to herself. Even Agatha's being a vampire spy would not derail her for long.

Agatha nodded.

"You'd do that for me?" Now that Agatha's motivations were in question, Sophronia was wise to double check.

Agatha nodded again, because she would. Because she would always consider them her friends, even if she had justifiably shattered that loyalty in them. And also because she kept her promises.

The moors stretched out before them and Agatha was already considering how to slip away from the long line of students and get to that one inn where a certain toocharming tavern owner with expensive taste in waistcoats had a fast horse and a system in place for reaching London at speed.

"It won't be as quick as we'd like," she said, because she was not a particularly good horsewoman.

"It never is," Sophronia replied.

Agatha nodded and slipped away to do Sophronia's bidding one last time. She could feel Pillover's eyes on her, and she knew he tracked her, even as she used every art she had to fade into the shadows of the gorse. Even as Sophronia was issuing him orders, Pillover's gaze weighted her shoulders. But then, she had never been able to completely hide from him before, and she had never really tried.

Why start now?

CHAPTER FIVE
THE END OF EVIL

New Year's Day 1854 ~ the most select drawing room in all of London

Pillover assessed Lord Akeldama's drawing room. It was opulent in every possible way, which was to be expected. *Every* possible way, including intellectual opulence. There were gilt-edged maps rolled and arranged in a wide gold lacquer caddy and the same again containing aether charts. There were a great many beautiful books, chosen, one assumed, for their attractive spine designs and not for the strength of their content. However, upon closer inspection, they showed wear and use and no little thought in theme and collection. Not all of the room was artifice. Some of it was about function. Or perhaps it was more that Lord Akeldama's world generally embraced both.

Pillover, of course, gravitated towards the books. History mostly. There was no way to ask Lord Akeldama directly about the nature of his choices – it being broad daylight, the vampire was still abed. A pity, because Pillover only really enjoyed talking to people when they could discuss books. Lord Akeldama probably considered historical analysis *fictional light reading* and found it highly entertaining.

He wondered if the vampire had ever met Catullus. And if so, what he thought of the poet. Regrettably fascinated by the female form, most likely. Prone to hyperbole and fits of the sulks. In Pillover's limited experience, poets were best confined to the written word. What a pity he did not currently have the opportunity to ask.

In the absence of their vampire master, a drone ignominiously named Pilpo was hosting their spontaneous gathering. The assembly, laboring under somewhat extraordinary circumstances, consisted of himself, Agatha, two lady professors from the now nonexistent finishing school, several sooties, their cat, and his repulsive sister.

A short while later it also included Sophronia, who stumbled in from a long sleep looking decidedly the worse for her adventures alone aboard a dirigible. Adventures, as Pillover often said, had *consequences*. She had managed, during the course of the previous evening, to see off all interlopers but had also reduced the school to utter rubble shortly after falling out of it and landing in a vegetable patch.

Dimity ran to Sophronia the moment she walked into the drawing room, making a series of cooing noises and sounding exactly like a drowning pigeon.

"Sophronia, my dearest, what you've been through! Such suffering." Dimity had no more idea of the particulars than anyone else, but she liked to talk that way.

Pillover gave an audible snort. It was audible because he *meant* it to be.

Agatha joined Dimity in attending to Sophronia. Pillover was pleased that she did so with considerably less fanfare than his sister. If anything, she looked somber and sad. She took one of Sophronia's hands briefly in both of hers, pressing fervently. "Welcome, oh returning hero."

Pillover winced. Maybe even his grounded Agatha could be effusive given the right set of incentives, like schools falling out of skies.

"Oh, do stop, both of you." Sophronia dipped her head but was clearly delighted.

Pillover joined them, grinning. Girls were so much more generous with compliments than boys. Or maybe it was just him. He never knocked schools out of skies, or did anything much deserving of a compliment.

Agatha glanced at him, lashes lowered, and instantly proved his point by heaping praise on his head. "Pillover is also a hero. Did you know, Sophronia?"

Pillover felt his face go hot and tingly. That had not been his design in joining them.

His sister, of course, being the human form of a toothache, said not at all quietly, "Oh, I say. He is no better than a mangel-wurzel."

Shockingly, it was one of the teachers who came to Pillover's defense, agreeing with Agatha. The one who looked a little like a nun was sitting and observing their touching reunion. "He is indeed. He helped us escape. Bunson's was working with the Picklemen. Agatha's young man here helped free Lady Linette and myself. We were locked up. In a boy's school! It was most embarrassing."

Which was true, if a bit exaggerated. Pillover hadn't done all that much. Just waited for the others to go about their evil matters and then snuck about setting everyone free. He might be bookish, but he was still a boy accustomed to sneaking. He'd had to become somewhat competent at *the sneak*, being Sophronia's friend, Dimity's brother, and Vieve's stalwart companion. Sneaking was practically mandatory under those circumstances (bookish or not bookish).

The professor's dig about his belonging to Agatha made his face feel as though it were actually on fire, but he enjoyed it too much to object. Besides, he was too embarrassed to call attention to the honorable title of *Agatha's young man*.

Sophronia said, "Dear Pill, will this diminish your standing at school?" She seemed genuinely worried.

Pillover was touched by her concern. "Not at all. If anything, it will increase it. Bunson's isn't the kind of place to hold a dose of traitorous sneaking about against a fellow. They'll probably elevate me to Reprobate Genius, which is one step closer to true Evil." He wasn't sure of this, but it was a possibility, and he didn't want the girls to worry about him. Especially not Agatha. He would be fine at Bunson's without them nearby. He wouldn't like it, but the world would be better for having them out in it. He truly believed that.

"Where's Vieve?" Sophronia asked him.

Pillover shrugged. "She said she wasn't up for learning about the large-scale destruction of technology. She said it would be necessary, that you would see to it, but she doesn't want to know details." Also, he privately suspected that his friend didn't like vampires and wanted as little to do with them as possible. Even Lord Akeldama. Especially Lord Akeldama. As vampires went, he was one of the worst best examples of the species. Pillover got distracted thinking about why that might be and didn't rejoin the conversation until Sophronia called him by name.

"I thought you didn't enjoy adventures. Why did you do it, Pill?"

"Did I say I enjoyed myself?" he said as sharply as he could. Did she think he was becoming like them? Like any one of them? Agatha and Sophronia and Dimity were all very different personalities, but they all had one thing in common. They eagerly played games of status and supernaturals. They actively liked involving themselves in political nonsense and societal excrement.

Pillover glanced at Agatha. She was hanging her head so he couldn't make out her expression.

"Well, we were happy to have you." Sophronia was trying not to smile for some reason.

"So you should be," he replied, well knowing his part to play in their group dynamic. He let himself sink back into dour grumpiness. "I won't do it again," he muttered darkly, too low for most of them to hear.

His sister, egged on by his expression, tutted at him. "Heaven forfend you enjoy yourself, you wombat."

Agatha said nothing, although he caught her looking at him once or twice. She seemed pleased or even smug for some reason.

Dimity then demanded Sophronia give them a full accounting of her adventures aboard the airship and how it had come to die. They all settled about Lord Akeldama's drawing room for some delicious tea, some decent comestibles, and some adequate oration. Pillover, of course, chose a seat near the bookshelf.

Sophronia was, no doubt, a most excellent spy, but she was not a particularly good storyteller. She left off important details and gave away too many others. Although Pillover supposed that might be by design or training.

Idly, he pulled one of the books off the shelf. Roman history. He flipped through it, amused to find that someone had written notes in the margins. In classical Greek. Which Pillover also read (although his Greek was nowhere near as good as his Latin). Instead of being notes on the contents, these proved to be rather amusing commentary on the behavior of the historical persons involved, in the style of a playbill critique. He sipped his tea and ate a sardine sandwich which someone, maybe Agatha, had passed over to him when he wasn't looking. Did she know how much he liked sardines? Very thoughtful of her.

At some point the doorbell chimed and Pilpo disappeared, only to return with yet another Geraldine's girl. Pillover supposed he really ought to think of them all as ex-Geraldine's girls now. This one was blonde, refined, a little too pretty, and definitely too aware of all three. Her name, which he recalled with some effort, was Monique. She clutched one of the more popular news-rags, which made Pillover focus more firmly on his book in disgust. He tried to hide the fact that he'd dripped sardine oil on one of the pages.

Monique appeared to object to the fact that the editors of said paper had been given evidence irrefutably exposing the Picklemen and their secret society. Pillover thought this was all very well and good, since he'd never have to deal with those blighters again. The world was always better off for one less secret society.

The implication was that Sophronia had provided said evidence to Dimity and that his sister had seen its distribution to the popular press. Which explained what his sister had been up to while he was busy saving her professors.

"Lord Akeldama may feel similarly," Pilpo said at that juncture, implying that the vampire also would object to the involvement of the gossip rags. But it was the way he looked at Agatha that caught Pillover's attention. She looked unhappy, as if something about this situation had put her on the spot. Was Agatha supposed to have gotten hold of that evidence instead of his sister? Given it to Lord Akeldama instead of the press?

Spycraft was awfully messy work.

Monique was talking with her former professors about matters chaotic – mobs in the streets, mechanicals being destroyed, and that kind of thing. All the consequences of Sophronia's actions and Dimity's distribution of the evidence. The two of them had caused quite the little revolution. If Pillover were disposed to be impressed by such poppycock, he would have been. He wasn't so he, well, wasn't. He went back to the very amusing Roman history book.

Monique eventually left as abruptly as she had arrived, and the girls and their professors continued to sip tea and talk. The conversation eventually settled upon the fact that, so far as the two teachers were concerned, all three girls were now considered *finished*. Which Pillover gathered was the equivalent of matriculating with distinction.

Agatha and Dimity were even praised for a "daring charge across the countryside on wolf-back."

Agatha smiled a smile Pillover hadn't seen before. "We are really finished? Truly?"

His sister looked like she was about to cry. Pillover very much hoped not. Even if they were happy tears, he was certain he'd misplaced his handkerchief and he hated it when anyone cried.

Dimity clasped her hands together. "We really are finished? Mummy will be so proud."

Dimity had always wanted to please their parents and never thought she would be able to. Like him, she hadn't an evil bone in her body. Their insisting that she become an intelligencer was a bit rich, really. So far as Pillover could tell, his sister had very little of it – intelligence, as it were. Yet Dimity had, against all expectations, managed it, despite his doubts and her flaws. Despite their parents' insistence on a lifestyle ill suited to her character. Despite her own reservations. He supposed he had to give her credit for that, and credit for actually trying in the first place. He did not intend to try at Bunson's, never had. He had years more to get through before he could safely escape to a respectable institute of higher learning, one that did not specialize in explosives and illegal activities. He was doomed to fall short of his parents' expectations, so he was somewhat relieved that at least one of their offspring would make them happy. He was also a little sad. There had been a part of him that anticipated a future where both he and Dimity would prove filially disappointing. Now he was alone in this pursuit.

He wasn't sure Dimity herself would ultimately be happy with the path she was now on. Not in the way that Sophronia and Agatha would be happy. His sister didn't want to be an intelligencer (she wasn't stealthy by nature), but she would do it because it was expected of her.

He should have been happy to have witnessed his sister's success. But all he really remembered was Agatha's fake smile and the mixed hope and fear that she was hiding behind it.

~

1854 - 1858 ~ Bunson and Lacroix's Boys' Polytechnique, Devonshire

Pillover had made it through his first four years of evil genius school mostly with the help of his sister and her friends, who had become mostly his friends by the end. Or to be more precise, he had made it through with the *distraction* of them. And the hope of them. The fact that they were out there in the world while he was busy hiding from his tormentors in the forgotten stairwell of the old root cellar, or pretending to be living in some other place and time reciting Latin in his head under the covers of his meager bed.

Unfortunately (or fortunately, given the state of his pining interest in a certain older redhead who likely thought of him as no different from a kid brother, if she thought of him at all) Dimity and her friends were completely absent from his life for the next four years.

Occasionally Vieve would mention some bit of information about one or another of them. But it never involved Agatha. No doubt anything she did or accomplished was done so far in the shadows that no one noticed it at all. He got sporadic letters from his sister, but she was very busy in town, and they had none of her old chattiness – she rather forgot about him. Which was fair – most of the time he forgot about her, too. Still, he always opened them eagerly and read them several times, sparse as they were, because he knew that Dimity and Agatha had set up house together in town, for ease of finances and autonomy. Agatha had succeeded in acquiring the independence she'd always craved, with no father, brother, or husband monitoring her liberty. Only one vampire, and Agatha's patron was nothing if not disinterested in the details of her activities. Pillover got the impression that Lord Akeldama issued instructions, and then waited for results with absolutely no care as to how those results were achieved. Unfortunately, he had to entirely guess at Agatha's feelings and actions because even living together, Dimity wrote very little about her quiet friend. Agatha did not inspire verbosity, even in his sister.

For the next few years Pillover and Vieve suffered under the barbs and fists of the leftover Pistons. They now boasted imprisoned Picklemen fathers and cherished, understandably, a rather large grudge against Pillover in particular. He and Vieve spent a great deal of time running and hiding. They helped each other whenever possible and in countless ways, from defense to distraction to bruise balm and bandages. As a result, Pillover would remain a steadfast and true friend to the wily French inventor in payment for all the times that tiny fearless frame had tricked boys bigger and meaner than both of them into leaving off some horrible bit of mischief.

Then, when Pillover was around sixteen, something changed.

One would think it was Pillover taking steps to improve himself, but actually it was more simple than that – he finally grew up. Despite himself. The oversized greatcoat suddenly fit him perfectly. Much to his surprise, and everyone else's, he also grew muscles. He certainly hadn't earned them, unless lifting books counted, but he got them anyway. Vieve taught him, mostly, how to use them because she'd spent time with sooties, and sooties knew how to fight. It took only one very fast, very hard punch (which split his knuckles and hurt his hand dreadfully) and things at school were suddenly a great deal better for both of them.

No one cared to trouble Pillover if Pillover was too much trouble back. He took that lesson to heart and started carrying around with him a small fire-starter kit, of Vieve's invention, and randomly striking flame and gazing into it as if he were an occultist. If someone came too near, he shoved the flame at them. When boys said anything cutting or teasing, he just stared at them. He dug his hands deep into his pockets and left one shirttail untucked, and half his waistcoat unbuttoned. He got a reputation for being not just gloomy and lacking in conversation, but for a touch of insanity. A rumor circulated that he was holding onto reality by only one frayed thread.

And that was it.

He was left alone.

Which wasn't ideal, but was better than the alternative. So he weathered his final years at Bunson's as an uncouth, sloppy madman with only Vieve for company.

After he graduated, he faced his parents squarely and disappointed them horribly by admitting to the fact that he did not want to be an evil genius and carry on the family business. Instead, he wanted to attend Oxford and study the classics.

Since he had reached his majority, they could not stop him from doing exactly that. And they didn't, spending the rest of their lives profoundly disappointed by the fact that their only boy child had grown into a perfectly decent, and regrettably ordinary, member of academia.

CHAPTER SIX
COMING OUT AFTER MIDNIGHT

April 1858 ~ The start of the London season

There was nothing particularly special about this ball, it was an ordinary private affair like many others. But Mr Pillover Plumleigh-Teignmott had traveled by train from Oxford especially to attend, because his sister Dimity was officially coming out into society and he was minded to be a good and decent brother. After all, he was the only one she had. His attendance had nothing at all to do with the fact that Miss Agatha Woosmoss was also making her debut. Miss Woosmoss wasn't doing it as loudly as Dimity, but she was doing it. Apparently, her father expected it of her.

The two young ladies had already been in London for several years, living a respectable life on the fringes of society with an estimable chaperone of excellent reputation and blessedly heavy slumber, who Pillover knew had been provided by Lord Akeldama at no little expense. But to really conduct their more covert business, they needed to circulate freely in the drawing rooms and ballrooms of high society. To do that, they needed to be *out*.

Someone was, of course, sponsoring his sister, but not to the extent that she might throw herself a ball, and their parents were certainly against any such expense. So Pillover was unfamiliar with the house, the hostess, and the guests. Indeed, he had no idea who his sister's patron was. Governmental, he suspected, from the meanness of her expense account and the frequency of her paperwork, both of which she was prone to complain about in her infrequent letters. She wouldn't tell him the particulars – she wasn't stupid, and he hadn't asked, because he wasn't stupid either – but he knew she had never stopped working. Like Agatha. Both of them were always working. Agatha for Lord Akeldama and Dimity for... someone else.

Pillover was working, too, but his work involved studying ancient words and places, and he was happy enough to have been well out of their extraordinary affairs. But that didn't stop him from wanting to see them again in person.

See *her* again.

He couldn't spot Agatha, though. He suspected he wouldn't be able to this time until she came to him. He had lost the knack and she'd had four more years to perfect the way she disappeared into wallpaper.

He spotted his sister right away, though. She was making no attempt at subterfuge. That would defeat the purpose of officially coming out, besides which, stealth had never been her style. Dimity sparkled her way into gathering information. She took center stage and charmed the world into submission. She was a great deal more like Lord Akeldama in this, which Pillover supposed was one of the reasons the vampire hadn't recruited her. Lord Akeldama already had plenty of her ilk in his stable, including himself.

Agatha, on the other hand, was a different creature entirely and she would go where he and his drones could not. She was probably there now.

Dimity was wearing some overly ruffled gown that was, no doubt, to the very height of current fashion. Pillover had to admit that the blue color suited his sister, as did the pearl strand (modest, as was required of a young girl at her first official event). Dimity was a touch old to make a debut, but she looked younger and she was intent on starting as she meant to go on – lying ruthlessly to society about her age. Dimity had fresh flowers in her hair, which was arranged in a demure style. She looked well (slightly out of character, but well). She did the family proud... if such a thing were his by right to be proud of. His sister's looks, he rather thought, were not his property, and should not, perforce, contribute to his consequence, despite the fact that he'd had countless gentlemen over the years compliment her to him. As if having a pretty sister somehow added to his worth. After all, Pillover knew for a fact that while Dimity was a silly bint, she had many fine qualities and no few abilities well beyond a prettily turned ankle and dewy complexion.

He made his way over to her and bowed a greeting.

"Brother dear!" she cried, because he was a handsome younger man who had approached her openly without introduction. She must protect her own reputation.

He cleared his throat and said equally loudly, "Sister. You look very well this evening."

"As do you. You've grown again."

He nodded. "I do believe I shall stop now."

"Oh, is this something you can control? How very precocious of you."

Pillover did not dignify that with an answer. "Have you a lead for the first dance or is that my duty to discharge to the best of my poor abilities?"

"Darling brother, that you would even consider inconveniencing yourself on my behalf does me great honor, but – and I beg you not to take this amiss – I am a little bemused that you do not trust in the fact that my dance card is already entirely full. This ball has been underway for a full three quarters of an hour."

Pillover tilted his head in acknowledgment of a point well served. "My mistake. Of course it is full. Then who am I to dance with, and what am I to talk about with them?"

"Oh my dear, you *have* grown." Dimity twinkled in approval, which was startling. She so rarely approved of him. "And how is Oxford?"

"Exactly as stuffy and old and miserable as you might expect, like bread fit only for the ducks."

"And you adore it, of course."

He offered her his arm and they began to circulate about the room. She pointed out a few young ladies worthy of his attention and suggested some topics of conversation, which Pillover knew meant he was to quiz them for information to the best of his limited abilities. She pointedly introduced him to all the chaperones as *my dear brother, still at Oxford*, so they would know both his age and social standing. He knew that he cut a fine figure, but his status as a nascent academic rendered him unthreatening and effectively removed him from the pool of prospective husbands. This placed him firmly in the category of *safe but inconsequential* dance partner. No ladies would set their caps at him this evening, thank heavens. But he would be expected to do his duty by the wallflowers, youngest sisters, and less desirable misses. The mothers would be grateful to him and attentive to Dimity as a result of any such efforts. Pillover might eschew social gatherings, but he was very well aware of his role.

He kept his eyes open for one redhead, but never did spot her.

They finished circulating back near the refreshment table, where Dimity engaged in some light punch and even lighter flirtation while he determined how to ask her the only question that mattered.

Meanwhile, he acted chaperone to the best of his ability. Pillover was a great deal younger than most of the gentlemen present, certainly all of the ones who paid any attention to his sister. As such, he was regarded as more of an interloping schoolboy, but they accorded him some respect as brother, even if he himself had no social cachet.

He did his best, but for Pillover that involved looming and glowering whenever Dimity sent him that pleading look of hers. Sometimes it worked, mostly it didn't, and then she had to shake herself free of whichever gentleman was annoying her. Fortunately for both of them, Dimity had been trained in nearly a dozen ways to extract herself from an uncomfortable conversation and just as many ways to kill the gentleman in question should he become too boring.

For his own part, Pillover grumpily fended off various young ladies who would keep coming up and twittering at him. Young ladies always did that to Pillover. It was vexing. He sneered at them, but this only made it worse.

The musicians began to prepare. The hum of excitement amongst the young people increased.

"Are you going to ask, brother dear?" Dimity said finally, looking up at him with a pert expression during a lull.

"I assume she is here?"

"Of course. And you haven't spotted her yet, have you? Even though you've been looking this entire time." Dimity tapped her fan against her cheek, coy. "She's sitting over there, next to that potted fern under the painting of whatever that is."

"A horse?" suggested Pillover.

"Oh, is it? I rather thought it might be a dog."

"Or a dirigible with fur and three legs."

"Ghastly, isn't it?"

"Very. The set is forming."

Dimity nodded, flicking her fan open to hide the fact that she was laughing at him.

Pillover gave a half bow. "I'll be about my duties then, my dearest sister. Wiggle a glove when you need me, or whatever it is you do. I, at least, should be relatively easy to spot."

"I'll simply look for a group of silly young misses with you, too tall and very pained, at the center."

Since that was a fair assessment of his evening plans, Pillover strode away. Taking advantage of the last opportunity to cross the dance floor directly before the ball officially began.

He kept his eye on the hideous painting because he was tolerably certain that he wouldn't notice Agatha until he was directly in front of her.

"Miss Woosmoss, good evening." He bowed, abbreviated and informal. Then he collapsed into the empty seat next to her without invitation.

"Mr Plumleigh-Teignmott. How did you find me?"

"You are perfectly in form, don't worry. My sister gave away the game by pointing you out. Or, to be more precise, by pointing out the painting."

"Did she indeed? Little traitor."

"Am I unwelcome, then?"

"Certainly not. Well, not at the moment. It's merely that you are rather noticeable. To young ladies in particular."

Pillover wondered if she included herself in that mix. Probably not. "It's a curse." He explained, morosely.

"You're unpleasant and sullen. It's most appealing."

He stared at an ink stain on his glove. "Because *that* is logical."

"Who could ever make logic of human affection?" wondered Agatha. "Not even the Greeks."

Which was true, actually. Since his own affection for her indeed defied logic.

"Shall we dance, then?" He made the offer sound as reluctant as possible.

"Not the opening set, no. Far too many people are watching. You may have the third, if you like. Go make some young, impressionable miss just out of plaits the happiest girl at the ball."

"You overestimate my consequence," he grumbled.

"Not to a young, impressionable miss, I assure you. See that one there? She's the daughter of a very well regarded diplomat. She has recently displayed an unfortunate interest in marine wildlife and this is her first season. Go dance with her. Ask her about jellyfish."

Pillover stood, made his bow. "If you insist. See you for the third. Jellyfish, you say?"

"Jellyfish."

He nodded and mooched off.

The young lady in question was better than many of her ilk in that she was not so chatty as she might be. However, she did become chatty once jellyfish were mentioned. Pillover minded it less when a chit prattled on about interesting subjects. It was when they succumbed to the lure of fans, or fashions, or, heaven forfend, *other girls* that Pillover rather lost his brains by way of a glazed expression.

He danced the next set with a young lady Dimity had asked him to flirt with. But she was one of those tragic cases who'd been instructed that the only safe topic was the weather. Pillover got nothing from her but an exhaustive account of how she was certain that there would be rain next week and what a pity to put such an early dampener on the picnic season. Pillover didn't realize there *was* a picnic season, which he said, and which seemed to embarrass the young lady into silence for the rest of the set.

His dance with Agatha, therefore, was a welcome relief.

"You already look quite pained." She hooked up her train to take position.

"You know I loathe these events."

"I do. Why did you come, then?"

"It's your official coming out, you and Dimity. How could I miss it?"

"Mr Plumleigh-Teignmott, don't pretend to be a good brother."

"I am not, I assure you! Either pretending or a good brother. Or your pretend brother, for that matter."

Agatha lowered her lashes and then looked up at him through them. "No, I know."

It was a flirtation, a blatant one. He found himself suddenly noticing the rose-petal softness of her cheek and the white length of her throat. The way her lashes fell, darkened for the evening, since normally they were red, like her hair. She was made soft and vulnerable with that one motion. It caught him up, pressed into his chest, made him ache. For a moment Pillover basked in it. He lowered his head to catch her gaze or her scent – to catch *something*, any part of her that she wished to parcel out.

He jolted in shock.

This was something she'd never done to him before. Something she'd never used on him. It was manipulation. It felt wrong, slimy somehow. That she'd use her education on him in such a manner. But also that she felt the need. As though somehow she'd forgotten that they were different, or at least Pillover had always *thought* they were different. She did not have to make use of him through artifice. She did not have to manipulate or force him to do anything. She could just ask. All of them, Dimity and Sophronia too, they only had to ask. She should know him – them – well enough to realize that.

It made Pillover angry. "I've seen you train. I know that you can make me feel all kinds of ways. Why would you use the eyelashes on me? What purpose does that serve?"

"Did I do that?" she sounded genuinely surprised.

He gave her a heavy stare from beneath dark brows, annoyed with her as he never had been before.

She returned to herself with a blink. Her eyes widened. "It wasn't intentional, I assure you."

"Practicing?"

"Instinct. Sorry, Mr Plumleigh-Teignmott." She sounded a little like she might be upset with herself.

"I am not your mark. I am your friend." Pillover was still hurt. He didn't want her thinking of him as being like every other boy, or any other boy. Even if she did it by accident or instinct.

"Are you indeed?"

"Did you forget or just never know?"

"You are my friend's brother. Was it more? Did I miss something?" She was pulling back for some reason. At the time he'd thought it was her shock at what she'd done. Later he would come to understand that it was shock at her own feelings. She'd flirted because it was her training to do so, but what had caused her to flirt was a desire for him to notice her. That had been the first crack in her armor, the crack he had always been looking for, and he had taken it entirely amiss and lashed out. She'd reacted by challenging their friendship in order to withdraw more. The memory always made him wince, for all that he now knew these were the natural mistakes of youth.

At the time Pillover hid his hurt, believing that all their history together had meant more to him than to her. Believing that it had all meant more to him than it had to *any* of them – their adventures all those years ago now. He was younger. He lived a quieter life. Perhaps he thought more of them (and of Agatha in particular) as companions than they ever had of him.

It was a terrible thing to realize that not only his affection but also his friendship had been one-sided.

He retreated into facetiousness. "Perhaps as time goes on you will allow me to improve my status from acquaintance to something more significant."

"Perhaps." Agatha wince-smiled. "It's unlikely."

"How can you say that?" Pillover felt his eyes tighten.

She rubbed at her collarbone with one gloved fingertip. "I hope never to be around long enough for you to have the opportunity." She didn't want him to care.

He wondered if she were being intentionally cruel or if this was the honesty of a kind of friend. Then he wondered if she was running towards or away from something.

"Do you travel soon, then? I thought you were busy making your debut. The season has only just begun."

"I meant to imply the future. When you are grown and I am established." Her eyes flashed suddenly over his shoulder. "Backwards and to the left, six steps."

Without questioning her, he moved their dance in the direction indicated.

This brought them close to a long mantelpiece decorated with a becoming display of pretty but expensive little objects. Agatha snaked out a hand, sliding a small coin from a tiny pile. Just one. She left more of the same behind.

AMBUSH OR ADORE

They were tokens of some kind. Brass. Stamped with a squiggly design, like a funny sort of flower.

He didn't ask her what it was or why she'd only taken one, but simply whirled her on to the floor and back towards her original corner of the room. They finished their dance in silence, Agatha contemplating a future and Pillover still stuck in the past.

Pillover stayed the full length of the ball, but he did not spot Agatha again, let alone dance with her. He insisted, however, on going home with Dimity to spend the night in their spare room rather than at his club.

Agatha did not return with them.

~

April 1858 ~ The most select drawing room in all of London

Lord Akeldama's front parlor hadn't changed much over the years. It was still opulent and grand. Perhaps it had evolved in nuances and details – to keep up with some of the trends in interior decoration – but in essence it remained the same. Rather like the good vampire himself. Agatha was dissatisfied with all of it – the house, the vampire, and herself. She knew that this was because she'd had to warn off Pillover in the worst possible way, to protect him from herself and her lifestyle. But she'd also done it to protect herself from him. She wasn't happy with anything right now because she felt like a coward. Self-recrimination was not a good state to be in when facing a vampire.

Agatha passed Lord Akeldama the metal button, carefully, as if it were fragile. It was of a military style, brass, with a stamp on it – actually quite durable. On first inspection the design seemed to be a flower of some kind, but closer examination revealed it to be an octopus. It was not the design that had attracted her into collecting the button – it had been her observations of those who picked one up. Gentlemen of a very specific ilk – smart, well situated, and scientifically inclined. Someone was recruiting, and using these buttons to do so.

Lord Akeldama examined the design through the lens of a monocle that he did not need. "*This* makes you believe that we have a new secret society in town?" He turned it around. His hands were a little closer to skeletal than graceful, which was probably why he so often wore gloves, even at home. But not tonight.

"I believe that is the most likely explanation. This is certainly a token of some kind. It could allow entrée into a new gaming establishment. Or a brothel. Except that the focus was so clearly on scientists. Men with a certain spirit of individualism and a reputation for less savory experimentation and lax moral fiber."

"Scientific thought is becoming more and more lucrative. And more dangerous." The vampire ran a thumb over the texture of the octopus.

"And more political," added Agatha. "The removal of the Picklemen has left a void."

"You think *that* is what is happening, petal?"

"I think men like to gather in groups small enough so they might pretend superiority to those who are not members of the group. Intellectuals are no more or less susceptible than any other men in this respect."

"And you did not catch the distributor of the buttons?"

"I did not."

Lord Akeldama nodded. He was not upset. He knew how these situations worked. "We need someone on the inside, little heliotrope. Unfortunately, none of mine right now are equipped to join this *particular* breed of club. Academic inclination is not a trait in young gentlemen that interests me overmuch."

Agatha tilted her head. "Because they lack imagination or because you do?"

He chuckled. "Probably both. Although had I truly lacked imagination I would never have recruited you, now would I, my darling *rose hip*?"

"I have a suggestion, but it would take many years to come to fruition. And the person I have in mind would be working *with* me, not *for* you. Nevertheless, I think I know who should get this brass octopus button."

"I am intrigued. You so rarely advocate working with anybody else." Lord Akeldama placed the button on a sideboard and turned, tilting his head in that way of his, examining her face too closely.

Agatha kept her expression dispassionate. "I would need to travel to France to see this done. And, as I said, fruition might take some time. The individual I'm considering is still young and in university."

"I don't object to a long game, you know that, *peony pod*. I have, after all, nothing *but* time."

"You would be willing to send me to France?"

"Is that your *true* design in recommending this tactic, sweet pea?"

"Possibly. I have always desired to travel."

"Sometimes, Miss Woosmoss, I wonder if I underestimated you." His sudden use of her name was jarring, but Agatha was accustomed to the way he talked. When he spoke without affectation it meant he was thinking of something else.

"If it makes you feel any better, my lord, I often think exactly the same about you."

He quirked a brow. "Very well, I will arrange passage to France. Paris, *mon petit chou*?"

She nodded. "The university is somewhere outside of it, but I can make my own way there."

"You speak French, do you, *mon trognon*?"

"Of course, my lord. I did, after all, go to finishing school."

"Very well, I shall leave this in your more than capable hands, *ma mignonne*."

"There is one additional thing."

"In connection with the brass octopuses? Or have you another game in play?"

"The octopus. A local matter, another long game."

"Another acquaintance you wish to recruit?"

Agatha considered Pillover's disappointed face that very evening, when they'd been dancing together. His hand, firm and sure on her waist, and the way his fingers had twitched when she told him he meant little more to her than as Dimity's brother. When she'd told him they were not friends.

"A friend."

"But we have only the one button, *ma fleur*."

"True. But my tactic with this second one is to make it so that our octopuses witness a series of successes, and deem him worthy of recruitment."

"Aha. Instead of bringing the scientist to the octopus, the octopus will go to the scientist. Very clever, Miss Woosmoss. But why tell *me*? You know I prefer to allow you a certain level of autonomy in these matters. I do not need to know the particulars, only enjoy the results."

"Indeed. It is one of the reasons I like working for you, my lord."

"So why *are* you telling me, *ma petite pomme de terre*?"

"In this matter I very specifically need your help. Perchance do you have any untranslated Latin scientific texts? Medical texts would be best. But any philosophy, or essays on matters pertaining to the supernatural set and their biological makeup, would be useful. Accurate or inaccurate, it matters not. Although you should know, these would be published. That would be the objective."

Lord Akeldama nodded, entirely following her logic. "Your friend is a classicist, *ma jolie prune?*"

Agatha inclined her head.

"Yes, I think I have some documents just outdated enough to be irrelevant, but still interesting to modern scholars if they were to come to light over the next few years. Humans always find it so *fascinating* when the *so-called* ancients already knew something that modernists regard as the provenance of *current* intellectual thought. When do you require these texts?"

"Now."

Lord Akeldama picked up a little gold bell and rang it.

Agatha quickly faded behind one of the thick sapphire-blue velvet curtains, effectively disappearing from view.

A drone appeared in response to the summons. Lord Akeldama gave him exact instructions on where to find several scrolls and the young man left the room.

Agatha stayed hidden, for she did not know how long this would take. Lord Akeldama, who was patient and never made small talk – certainly not with her – stood and waited as well.

The murmur of voices indicated the young man's return and then the door was shut with an audible thud. Agatha reemerged.

Lord Akeldama had arranged himself to sit cross-legged and leaning to the side in a languid manner, at a small secretary desk in a corner of the room. A large stack of papyrus scrolls rested in front of him. He might have looked as if he were studying something, except the rolls were tied closed and he had an affected, desolate air about him. Lord Akeldama looked like the kind of man who had never read beyond the fashion papers in all his long life. It was a powerful illusion. Even with history stacked before him, written in a language he understood perfectly, he looked as if he and the scrolls were two parts of a different painting that had been haphazardly pasted together.

Agatha waited for him to notice her.

Eventually he did. "It really is remarkable, the way you disappear like that. I knew to look and I still couldn't see you."

"I would say it is a gift, but I trained for it."

"Quite right. One should be proud of that which is achieved through hard work and not merely ascribed to one by birth or natural talent. Although I think that in this regard, having met you as a child, it did start that way."

"Shall we say that I have *cultivated* it, then?" She suggested the term.

"*Wallflower* indeed, like a vine of invisibility, robust and *verdant*." He gestured at the scrolls.

She collected them and made them disappear into the secret pocket of her wide ballgown.

"I would urge you to have fun in France, Miss Woosmoss, but I think you are not the kind of young lady who seeks *fun*."

"I do have my own form of it."

"Quite right. There are as many forms of fun as there are ways to tie a cravat. And just like cravat knots, some entertainments are quite subtle and others quite vulgar, and most are a matter of personal taste unfortunately foisted upon the world."

Agatha shook her head at his flights of fancy. Sometimes the vampire spoke in riddles she thought were entirely constructed for his own amusement and not the enlightenment of others. But then, perhaps that was his fun.

"Good evening, Lord Akeldama."

He smiled, showing fang but only a little bit. It was a smile she liked, because there was the hint of threat to it. It reminded her that he was a predator. And it reminded her that she was getting out, still alive.

"Oh, have I been *dismissed* by *La Giroflée*?" he said, cheeky.

Ridiculous man, this was his house.

She flicked her hand at him and slipped from the room. She made her way through the kitchen and out the back door into an alleyway with no one the wiser for her having visited.

No one human, that is.

~

April 1858 ~ The least select parlor in all of London

Pillover had mixed feelings about Agatha and Dimity's small townhouse in London. The girls called it their Ha'penny Challet. It was homey, which he liked, but it was in London, which he hated. It always seemed to be cold and drafty and, as the years wore on, it felt less and less lived in as both girls spent more and more time away from it. But his first memories of it were generally positive because it was partly Agatha's home and he had been allowed into it.

Of course, his first time there was with his sister, not Agatha.

Pillover and Dimity had settled in the warm and slightly shabby parlor. The chaperone had long since retired to bed, having already partaken of a goodly amount of sherry.

Enough so that she had not worried, or perhaps even noticed, that Agatha was not with them on the return drive.

In the carriage, Dimity had explained to the woman without any effort that Agatha had left the ball early, overcome with a headache, and returned home well before them. The chaperone, whose name Pillover could not remember, was satisfied with this.

"Oh, I do not concern myself overmuch with Miss Woosmoss," she proclaimed, her words a touch slurred.

"Nor should you," approved Dimity.

"She is of little worry to anyone, poor creature." The chaperone shook her head sadly. "Not like you, my pretty dearie."

Dimity dipped her head in a parody of a blushing maiden. "You give me too much credit, Miss Corpugunt. Far too much."

"I assure you, I do not. The gentlemen find you broadly appealing, dearie. You have such fine qualities of spirit and appearance as to render your lack of fortune of little consequence. Miss Woosmoss is the opposite. Although her father is known to be well set up, her defects in looks and character render her not at all tempting, poor thing."

Pillover had slouched deeper into the carriage seat and sneered at the woman.

Dimity did not protest. It would do no good, as this was the part Agatha had chosen to play. Dimity was not going to protect her friend when this attitude was exactly what Agatha wished to encourage in others. After all, this allowed Agatha such things as complete autonomy of an evening. Because wherever Agatha had gone, it was certainly not home to bed with a headache.

Pillover sighed loudly.

Dimity took the cue. "Oh, brother dear, are you utterly exhausted?"

"Utterly. You overran me with young ladies of consequence and inconsequential chatter and I may never forgive you, sister dear." He grimaced at her.

The chaperone tutted at them for being so much siblings that they couldn't simply enjoy the end of a ball without arguing about it.

And as a direct result of their managing to maintain a steady bicker for the rest of the ride home, she retreated as soon as they arrived, and they were left in front of a cheery fire sipping an excellent bottle of claret and not really saying much, as they didn't have an audience.

It was peaceful.

Pillover had so rarely had any quiet times with his sister over the years. He was surprised to find he was actually enjoying himself. He wondered if Dimity was sobering in her old age or if she was just overly tired from the ball.

Agatha found them there when she finally returned home some hour or so later.

"You two look cozy." She wandered in and leaned against a bookshelf near the door, crossing her arms and staring at them with her head tilted. "You know, for once you actually look like siblings."

Dimity was on a settee with her full skirts taking up most of it. Pillover sat in the wingback chair usually occupied by the chaperone. There was nowhere really for Agatha to sit, unless she sat on Dimity's dress.

Pillover made to stand and give her the chair.

Agatha shook her head. "Stay. I prefer the rug in front of the fire." Suiting actions to words, she settled at their feet closer to the flames, like a cat. With her skirts spread out flat, it became instantly clear that there was a suspiciously large lump in one section.

Dimity was moved to comment. "What have you got there, then?"

Agatha fished about through the seam and into a large hidden pocket, extracting a seemingly endless series of what looked like very old scrolls. Papyrus, unless Pillover missed his guess (unlikely). They might be Egyptian, or Greek, or Roman in origin. Pillover was intrigued.

"They're for your brother," said Agatha, effectively rendering Pillover even more intrigued.

She handed him one.

He unrolled it carefully. Latin, some kind of scientific or medical text. Intriguing that it was untranslated, although it was not a topic that particularly interested him.

"Do you wish these passed along for translation?"

"No," said Agatha firmly. "I want you to translate and publish them yourself."

"This is not exactly my field of interest or expertise."

"I was hoping you would be open to making an exception. You would be paid. Rather well."

Pillover was pained. "Steady on. I'm not that hard up."

"They are all medical or scientific in nature and many concern the supernatural – vampires in particular. It would be wonderful if you could translate them over the next few years. Under your own name. Steadily, but without any sparkle."

"When have I ever added any form of sparkle to anything I do?"

Agatha gave one of her soft genuine smiles. "Fair point."

Pillover considered the true nature of the request. "You wish me to build a reputation in this particular field of translation. Why? The actual quality of the scientific thought herein is likely to be profoundly outdated. Centuries outdated, in fact." He smiled at his own joke.

"Ancient knowledge is still regarded with interest and favor – some might even say affection – particularly anything from the Romans featuring vampires."

"You want me established as a voice of authority. Why?"

She did not answer that. "Will it be too much of a bother? Distract you from your poetry work?"

Pillover did some mental calculations on his current classes and schedule. He thought his Latin professor might let him work on this kind of thing as part of his regular coursework. "Most likely not." He raised the scroll. "This is actually much easier to translate. Since the goal is precision, I must only find the correct words and put them in the correct order. Poetry is far more complicated because it is art and open to interpretation, you see?"

Agatha nodded, although she did not look as if she understood the nuance at all. "So you'll do it?"

Pillover nodded. He would. Because it was a connection to her and a favor for her, even though she was no doubt involving him in someone else's business. That was the way things were with Agatha, and Dimity, and their friends.

Pillover had only ever wanted a quiet life as an obscure scholar, but they would drag him into their messes no matter what he did. Even if it was translating a dry Latin treatise on – he glanced down at the scroll in his hand – the nature and depth of fang bite in dead drones.

Dimity observed this whole exchange with interest, swirling her claret in her glass, and occasionally examining the flames of the fire through the rim. "What are you up to, Agatha? Are you involving my brother in something evil?" There was an edge to her voice that Pillover had never heard before. For the first time in his life, he wondered if she actually worried about him. If she genuinely cared. He'd never considered the fact that his older sister might feel some measure of responsibility towards him.

What a silly notion. He shook it off.

"Only on the periphery. He's game, aren't you,

Pillover?" Agatha used his first name, which she never did in public. It made him feel warm all over. Of course he would do whatever she needed. Especially something so simple and so within his abilities.

Still, it would not do to be enthusiastic. "All I must do is translate and publish?"

"And you can take your time. It won't matter until you've finished with your education and returned to London and society."

"Who says I will be doing that?"

"Oh, won't you?" Agatha looked surprised, as if she could not conceive of anyone not wanting to live in London.

"I may come to town to visit, as I am doing now, but I do not intend to keep my own residence here. I never did. You both know I can't abide London for any length of time."

"Interesting decision. Well, either way, will you do the translations?"

"With pleasure."

"I may send you more, when I am able?"

"Please do. But you must also write."

"Write?"

"To me." Pillover was not above bargaining for information. It was, after all, the only currency Agatha really understood.

"About what?"

Pillover took a gamble. "Anything you wish, so long as it is about you and not someone else."

"You're very demanding all of a sudden."

"Now, now, who is asking whom to translate and publish Roman scientific texts? This is not my field of interest, remember?"

"Very well," Agatha agreed, albeit reluctantly.

"You promise," he pushed, because he was still young enough to push.

She wrinkled her nose at him. "I promise."

Dimity grinned at them both. "My darling brother, you can rest assured that Agatha always keeps her promises, even to someone as silly as you."

CHAPTER SEVEN
MINISTRATIONS OF AN ACADEMIC

1859 - 1862 ~ The least select parlor in all of London

Accordingly, over the next several years, they established a kind of pattern. When Pillover was free of university, or could find a ready excuse to satisfy the dons, he popped into London and stayed with Dimity and Agatha. If the season was in play, he did his due diligence as escort, to the delight of many an impressionable young lady of dubious taste.

In the ballrooms of London he appeared a glum, glowering, moody academic of great appeal and little interest. His sterling reputation as a translator of unquestionably dull Latin scientific treatises cemented his standing as a young man of deep thought and nothing more. Mr Pillover Plumleigh-Teignmott was an intellectual whose rudeness must be excused by a mind stuck in the past, but whose general appearance and disinterest in romance were considered highly desirable qualities in a young gentleman. He was welcome in all of the best drawing rooms and many of the more obscure ones. If some young ladies of his acquaintance happened to find out that he also translated romantic poetry, a great deal of which was highly salacious, this only added to his appeal.

Pillover was the kind of boy everyone fancied themselves in love with, partly because he was the same boy in the hearts of all the other young ladies in any given season. So far as the chaperones were concerned, he was a handsome devil, too young to be much of a threat. His lack of fortune might have rendered him dangerous but for his manifold disinterest in marrying for money (or for any other reason, for that matter). All this rendered Mr Plumleigh-Teignmott the ideal gentleman to invite to any gathering, merely to add to the decoration and make up the numbers at whist.

The young ladies assumed, from Mr Plumleigh-Teignmott's morose countenance, that he had been unlucky in love. Rumors circulated that he'd been deeply heartbroken by an older woman and would pine his whole life away unless some nice young miss rescued him through the strength of her devotion and high moral character. Accordingly, ladies persisted in falling in love with him most seasons, and Pillover persisted in returning to his Latin none the wiser for the hearts that he had broken, and they none the wiser for his utter indifference.

Over his years at Oxford, Pillover became rather known (amongst those who keep track of such things) for his work in the area of Roman vampire physiology, although he was considered rather green, and there was some argument over the scientific accuracy of his translations. Since these works were not the ones he cared very much for, Pillover was disposed to think of any minor controversy on the subject as adding to his consequence. Agatha, whenever he happened to mention this to her, always praised him for his efforts on her behalf. Which was all he really cared about. She kept the Latin scrolls coming, and they were just unique enough for Pillover to develop a reputation for having a special secret source, making him the envy of many.

Agatha's work was taking her more and more outside of London. It turned out she had an affinity for languages (living ones, not dead). Plus her innate wallflower skills worked in her favor, even in foreign lands. Sometimes when Pillover visited the small townhouse, there was only his sister and their increasingly doddery chaperone to welcome him. Those times he never stayed very long, opting to return to Oxford even if it was still term break, preferring the cold, solitary mustiness of his rented garret, his stacks of books, and his ever-present scrolls.

But when Agatha was in town, Pillover stayed as long as he could reasonably get away with. Dimity, who understood him better than either of them cared to admit, would leave him alone in the evenings, in the tiny parlor in front of the cozy fire, waiting for one redhead to return. And she did return, usually late, sometimes bruised, and often tired. Because she worked with the supernatural set, Agatha's hours were incompatible with daylight.

He did not mind waiting up for her.

They developed a pattern.

He reading late into the night, she coming back in the small hours, quiet and stealthy. She would settle as she preferred to, on the floor in front of the fire, so subtly that Pillover rarely noticed her arrival.

Then at some point, he would glance up from his book to enjoy the flames, and instead find her curled before them, hugging her knees into her chest and staring into the grate.

He would put down his book and resist the urge to stroke her hair. Instead, he would ask her softly how her evening had been. She would answer him with platitudes, because she could not tell him the truth. He would read between her words and hunt her face for signs of strain. He would check on the whiteness of her knuckles around her knees and note the depth of the stains on the hem of her skirts. He would take in any rips or tears. If she were bruised or cut, he would go find his sister's medical chest and silently tend to her injuries with plaster or balm. He never asked for permission, because no doubt she would refuse. Even though he was not sure he doctored very well, it was better that it was done at all, for she would not ask anyone else for help.

He tried not to think of those moments as *the times he got to touch her*. He did not want to hope for her to be injured. He knew her job was dangerous. She was very good at not being seen, but if for some reason she *was* seen, it was usually because she was in the wrong place at the wrong time, and trouble, by necessity, followed.

He worried about all the times she came home and sat in front of the fire without him. He worried about all the times she returned hurt and there was no one to fetch the medical chest. But he would never burden her with his concern.

Then, during the height of the season in 1862, Agatha announced that she would be leaving on another journey, but it would be very long this time. She was booked on a steamer across the Atlantic to New York City. She seemed excited about it. Pillover had never seen her so animated about anything.

"It is a glorious thing," she told him, staring into the fire. "He is finally allowing me to go properly abroad. I mean, I have been to France many times now, and even Italy once, but this is so much more."

"How is Vieve?" Pillover asked, genuinely curious. He

and his old friend from Bunson's corresponded sporadically, but they did not share many intellectual pursuits anymore, so they had little of substance to convey to one another.

"Proceeding apace," replied Agatha. "She will matriculate shortly after you do, I believe, even though she is younger. I think she'll join a secret society of scientists soon."

"How unfortunate. I do loathe secret societies."

"I know you do, Pill." Agatha had taken to calling him *Pill* over the years, since that was what Dimity called him, and they were family of a kind. Pillover both liked and disliked it. The intimacy was nice, the moniker was not.

"Secret societies make the world go round, though," she said.

Pillover wondered if she belonged to any herself. "Do they indeed? I rather thought that was gravity." He reached forward, touched her shoulder, daring. "And you are telling me this, why?"

She tilted her head and pressed her cheek to the top of his hand. A sisterly affection that made him feel unbrotherly and unsettled.

"I think that the same secret society may reach out to you soon. You have a reputation, long established, in certain scientific circles. To do with Latin translations and vampires and medical texts."

"Ah, you set me up. It's been years. You do play a long game, don't you?"

Agatha nodded against his fingers. He kept the hand on her shoulder very still, for fear she would remember it was there and brush him off.

"I am to say yes to joining, I take it?"

"If you don't mind."

"Of course I mind. As I already said, I do *not* like secret societies."

"I will write to you from America," she offered. Knowing it was his weak spot.

They corresponded often. Or, to be more precise, she wrote to him when she could, from wherever she happened to be at the time. The missive would arrive, postmarked from a place where he had no doubt she *wasn't* anymore. She never wrote to him when she was home in London. That wasn't part of their deal.

He had no idea what she thought of this arrangement. He was only glad that she abided by her long-ago promise. He kept all her letters in a funny little box that pretended to be a bookend on one of his many, many shelves. No one was the wiser for what was in that box, because no one ever visited his garret and no one ever would.

She turned to face him, the fire making a nimbus of her red hair. Pillover let his hand fall reluctantly from where it rested. She looked up at him from her spot on the rug. That rug had changed over the years, become thicker and fluffier, because Dimity, who did the decorating, knew how much Agatha liked to sit just there. The wingback chair, which was always Pillover's when he visited, now had a cushion he could prop behind his back, because he liked to lean forward when Agatha was around. And while he mostly did not touch, there was the chance that he might, and Dimity knew that, too.

Dimity, who always left them alone in the evenings. Partly because her work was more human oriented and daytime strategic, but also because they were (as she complained loudly to Pillover in order to make him blush) too focused on each other, or the fire, and long silences. She did not understand why anyone would stay up late doing nothing at all, not even cards.

Such as now, with Agatha just looking at him, gaze soft, a little smile lurking somewhere behind her eyes.

She had lots of different smiles, his Agatha. There were the ones she used professionally – many and varied and well executed. He rarely saw those anymore. If Agatha came with them to a ball, she disappeared quickly into other rooms not meant for dancing. There were small, shy smiles that were hers alone, not shared and jealously guarded. There were little lip twitches when she found something funny that no one else did. And sometimes she gave a half-lifted, painful wince, the smile of pain or loss. Those happened at the fireplace when she came back from some covert assignation, and stared a long time at the flames. That smile wasn't really a smile at all, but a means of siphoning away hurt. After she gave that smile, she always hid her face, as if ashamed to have had any reaction at all to her own suffering.

That was the smile Pillover caught, briefly aimed at him, that night. The next morning, before he was awake, she left him for another land.

It would be that smile he remembered. He was weirdly honored that she had shared it with him and, for once, had not dipped her head or turned away. But she still left, and he had a horrible feeling he would have to get used to both the smile and her being gone.

He was right. It would be ten months before he saw her again.

~

April 1863 ~ A garret in Oxford

Dimity's hand was still flowery, but the slant had become more pronounced over the years. This particular missive from his sister was distinctly lacking in chattiness. There was none of her usual prattle about people he did not know, and fashions he did not follow. Instead, it was just two lines.

Brother dear, I have to go away.
   Could you come and look after my plants for me?
   Yours etc., Dimity

Dimity didn't own any plants. But sometimes there was a wallflower under her roof.

Pillover packed that night. He left a note with the college steward for his professor informing him that there was a family emergency and that he would be gone to town for a week. He apologized deeply and said he would try to do some translation work while he was away.

He caught the morning train from Oxford into London.

His sister and Agatha being in their mid-twenties now, and his presence expected as escort in Dimity's case, it was generally assumed the town residence was actually owned by Pillover. A younger brother, transient though he might be, was sufficient to render the two ladies autonomous. The chaperone had been retired to the countryside with sufficient means to keep her in gin and stockings. The two not-so-young ladies were now thought of as near enough to spinsters to make no odds. Pillover supposed that being in their mid-twenties, society regarded them as quite long in the tooth for females of the species. Which seemed ridiculous to Pillover (but then, so was most of society).

Accordingly, with his sister gone and no chaperone, the house was dead quiet when Pillover arrived. The fire was cold in the grate and there was no one around, not even a charwoman.

He made his way through to the spare room, where he

tossed his bag, and then heard a muffled, chattering whimper. Greatly daring, he knocked at Agatha's door. When no one answered, he pushed inside.

She was tossing in bed, sweating and fevered. He sat on the counterpane to touch her forehead, finding it much hotter than he liked. Her eyes popped open. She tried to focus on his face, but struggled.

"Pill? That you?"

"That me. What's wrong with you?"

"Just sick."

"Not an injury gone septic?" If this were an infection, he would need to lance the wound and summon a surgeon.

"If I promise not, will you still insist on stripping me to check?"

Pillover made a face. "I am a gentleman. I will take your word for it. But promise me. Don't be stupid. If it is an injury, I should call someone to treat it."

Agatha sported a fresh scratch along her lower cheek and jaw and there were bruises on her neck, as if someone had tried to strangle her. "I'm only battered about a bit. This is a bad cold, nothing more."

Pillover narrowed his eyes at her. "You promise?"

"I promise."

"Well then, let me think. What do you need? Liquids of some sort. Broth? Hot water and lemon, perhaps? Brandy? Calf's foot jelly, isn't it? A cooling cloth, or do we sweat this out of you?"

By the time he'd finished coming up with possible treatments, Agatha's eyes were closed. She appeared to have drifted off into a feverish sleep.

AMBUSH OR ADORE

Agatha did not know how long she was ill. Her memories were all fevered dreams, hazy impressions of Pillover's worried face, and embarrassment at her own weakness. She awoke to lucidity at last, feeling weak as a new kitten, her throat on fire and her head aching, but at least her mind was clear again.

There was a weight on part of the blanket near her waist, and her hand was resting on something warm and breathing.

She craned her head to see.

Pillover.

So she hadn't hallucinated that part. Dimity must have written urging him into town. Term was in session – he shouldn't be here at all. Yet he must have been looking after her for however long she'd been ill.

He was sitting on the floor, his arms crossed on the bed and his face buried in them, sleeping. Her hand was on his shoulder.

She twitched it a bit and he jolted awake, rubbing his eyes like a child. They were red from lack of sleep. Agatha hoped he wasn't going to succumb to her illness.

He stood and stumbled slightly. No doubt his legs were numb from such an awkward position. He landed sitting on the bed next to her, and then leaned over to touch her forehead with gentle fingers.

"Your fever has broken at last. Are you sufficiently *compos mentis*?"

She nodded a tiny bit, too weak for much more, amused by his very Pilloverian way of putting it. "Water?" she croaked.

He helped her to sit upright and raised a cup to her lips. "Slowly. Little sips, or you'll start coughing again."

"I've been *coughing*?"

"Like a fire eater. But it's the fever that worried me most."

"How long?" she asked. No wonder she sounded raspy.

"Three days. I was going to fetch a physician today if it hadn't broken. You were adamant, no quacks. But I told you if you weren't better today I was overriding you."

"We seem to have had whole arguments that I do not recall." She finished the cup of water by slow degrees and he settled her back.

His eyes were worried and he reached to smooth the hair away from her forehead.

Agatha thought she must look a sight and smell a treat, with three days of sweating fever and no bath to speak of. Still, she liked that he was comfortable enough to touch her, that care and worry had blown away that part of him that always shied away.

"Do you want to sleep more, or could you eat a little something?"

Her stomach noticeably growled.

Pillover's lips twitched and he straightened up. "I have some chicken broth, or there's calf's foot jelly, or porridge, or bread and butter. What can you manage?"

She couldn't stop her smile. "All the foods of invalids that you have read about in books?"

"Are you laughing at me?"

Agatha found herself thinking, for the first time, that Dimity's little brother was actually rather sweet. She had always found him good looking, and she knew he was loyal, but as her tired and worried nursemaid he was also somewhat adorable – like a flustered raven, feathers ruffled but doing his best.

"Of course not, Pill. Some broth would be nice. And if I can manage that, maybe bread and butter after?"

"I don't have much more than that," he warned. "There

was nothing in the pantry when I arrived, and I haven't wanted to leave the house for very long, and there's only the butcher's and the bakery nearby. Oh, there's also plenty of milk. The milkman kept coming. I could make you some tea? Or—" He paused, considering. "Bread soaked in warm milk. Isn't that a healing food?"

Agatha chuckled. "I am not a hedgehog."

Pillover gave a curt nod. "Broth it is."

Something changed between them during the course of Agatha's ensuing convalescence. A certain intimacy was forced upon them, since she was too weak to even make it to the privy on her own. Pillover was forced to carry her most places and then stand outside the door while she committed acts of delicacy. It was embarrassing, but Pillover was, like his sister, deeply practical about certain things. He had a no-nonsense approach to the necessities of life. Agatha accepted that in this matter, and for a few days at least, she must lean on him. She had no other option.

The rest of the time she was too tired to do more than sleep, or lie staring at the ceiling. She could not focus sufficiently to read or write. Eventually, Pillover asked her if she would like to be read to. At least it was something to relieve the monotony of recovery.

"Will you read to me in Latin?"

"If you prefer." So he did that for a while.

After a few days, Agatha grew tired of her bed and tiny room and begged to be moved to the parlor for a change of scenery. So Pillover set up the settee with blanket and cushions and helped her to stumble over. He lit a cheery fire and it was almost like old times, except she was not in her favorite place on the rug.

He'd just cleared away the lunch things and was making himself comfortable in his own chair with the book they were working on – something dry and philosophical,

Cicero, she thought it was — when instead of opening and beginning to read as usual, he said, "You're looking a little better today. Your eyes are clearer and your cheeks have color."

"I'm feeling better. Do you need to leave soon? You must be in the middle of term. Will your professors be very angry with you for this unscheduled absence?"

"I told them it was a family affair. I'm assuming they will not boot me out in my final year of study for needing to tend to my sister. I can stay here a few more days, until you're on your feet again."

Agatha nodded. Sister was good. She could be sister.

He fiddled with the book in his lap. "I won't ask where exactly you were or how you came to be so ill, but you were gone a long time. Were you at least successful?"

She considered. It had been a long run — New York, Boston, up into Halifax tracking rumors of a wild pack, and then of something not quite wolf, only to return to civilization to find sickness rampant through the human population. Then that hellish crossing, knowing she was coming down with an illness and unable to stop it. "I don't know. I learned some things that I didn't know before, but not what I was sent there to retrieve."

"Fortunately, your master embraces knowledge for its own sake."

She bristled. "Fortunate indeed, but would we call him *master*?"

Pillover tilted his head.

Agatha had long since come to accept that of all the people in the world, Pillover and Dimity knew her business best. Dimity did not care, for she had her own concerns, and her own information to track down and extract. They were friends, but no longer confidantes. They could not afford to be — they did not serve the same agenda anymore. And Pillover? Pillover had no one to tell her secrets to. Agatha kept him in the dark as much as she could for his own safety. But when he said things like this, he revealed how much he had absorbed of her situation over the years.

"Is he not? Your lord, then? Or merely your employer?"

"How much am I under his control and to what extent do I owe him my loyalty? That would seem to dictate the proper title." She had been offended by the term *master*, but perhaps it was in fact the most accurate. She did bow first to Lord Akeldama's whims. Not that she had ever wished to object to his instructions. She was paid like any household staff, though. Now that the vampire had accepted that her brand of intelligencer could go into the field and meet with success, he was delighted to deploy her regularly in that capacity. And she was delighted to be deployed. But it did speak more to a master and servant arrangement than any other.

"I serve his will. So I suppose *master* is good enough," she said at last. Not happy to admit it, but feeling she owed Pillover something for her care, even if it was only a small window into her soul.

He nodded, put Cicero to one side, and leaned forward towards where she lay, piled up on the pillows that he had gathered for her.

"I always assumed you did it for the freedom of it, and yet you are his creature. Is it worth that price?"

Brave words for a young man who would never have to serve anyone. Who had always possessed his own autonomy, for all he did not know to value it. Men who had choices handed to them regularly misconstrued privilege for luck.

Agatha plucked at the knitted throw covering her legs up to her waist. "I am a twenty-five-year-old spinster and I have already seen more of the world than most anyone else in England."

"Yet you cannot tell anyone about what you have seen."

"That is not the point."

"No. I don't suppose it is."

"The point is simply to *see* as much of it as I can. I've never been much of a talker. Just because I do not share about my life, that doesn't mean I do not want to live it to my own tastes and preferences."

Because this was Pillover, he took her words as truth. "Even if you must live it hidden and constantly disappearing? How will you remember something you never get to share and only observe from the shadows?" And while he was alluding to her particular skill of fading into the background, she knew he was also referring to her habit of disappearing from his life for long stretches of time.

Did he feel abandoned? How silly would that be? There was nothing between them, no reason for him to hope she might linger. No agreement, unspoken or otherwise. To feel left behind, he must first feel as if he had justified claim to her time. But Agatha could have no other master than the one to whose tune she already danced, and even a vampire was better than a husband. At least her contract with Lord Akeldama had an end date.

"It is what I have always been good at." She chose to respond to the first kind of disappearing and ignore the second.

"How do you do it – your wallflower trick? I've always wondered."

She gave him a gift then. "In London, I actually keep track of the wallpaper favored by the most prominent hostesses in town. I have a transformation dress made up to match."

"That is…" he trailed off, at a loss for words.

"Quite expensive, and often not of a fabric suited to my complexion. But that is not the point. You'd never think it to look at me, but I own one of the largest and most extensive dress collections in all of London. It's just that they are all dresses that no one would envy me in, should they chance to see me at all."

"But it's more than just what you wear."

"Of course. There is how I do my hair, the way I sit, the way I move around a room. I can't ever stand out. There is an art to vanishing in plain sight."

"You must know a lot about the decorations and layouts of people's houses."

"And public buildings, too. Not to mention the light, and of course, access points."

"It's part of your job not to clash?"

"Are you being pert, Pill?"

"Never. I just find it odd how no one ever sees you."

"No matter how I dress, I will always be that chubby girl in the corner. So I trade on a certain deficiency in perception."

Pillover frowned. "I hate it when you do that – belittle yourself."

Brotherly devotion and protection colored his tone. He did not understand. It was likely that he never would. "The *truth* is my business, Pill. I can't afford to avoid applying it to myself. Even if you refuse to acknowledge it. I'm not ashamed of being plain. The way I look has allowed me to pursue the life I want."

"You are not plain, just deluded."

She loved him a tiny bit then, for his stalwart if obtuse devotion. "It's nice that you think so."

"Nice that I think you are deluded?"

"Yes, Pill. More Latin now?"

He nodded and resumed Cicero.

He departed London a few days later, when she could get up and move about without his assistance. And while Agatha was glad to have the place to herself again, she missed his voice rumbling out Latin, his quiet presence near the fire, and his soft hand on her forehead checking her temperature.

CHAPTER EIGHT
THE ART OF VANISHING

1864 ~ Oxford

Pillover left his student status behind with little fanfare and less drama. He moved from his garret to a tiny cottage and pursued further study under the same don, at the same college, in the same building as he had prior to matriculation. The only major change was that he now undertook the tutelage of youngsters exactly like his former self.

His reputation as an expert in the field of Latin translations now firmly cemented, and his work having continued apace in the arena of medical texts, he was formally invited to join a society known by the rather ignominious moniker of *the Order of the Brass Octopus*. He joined, and like any other secret society, the local chapter meetings seemed mainly composed of extremely long rituals of little consequence run by the loudest gentleman in the room, whose pomp and circumstance existed in inverse proportion to his intelligence. Much of the ceremonial aspect was conducted in Latin, but to Pillover's disgust, the collective pronunciation was abysmal (possibly because everyone but him was of a scientific, not linguistic, inclination). The food was indifferent, the timing of events inconvenient, and generally Pillover's belonging to the secret society seemed to benefit nobody. But he dutifully maintained his membership, and he dutifully attended all required assemblies, even as he assiduously declined all optional invitations or purely social gatherings. He was doing this for Agatha, but that did not mean he had to enjoy himself, or put in any more effort than the absolute minimum. He was a martyr to love, beautiful red hair or no red hair, thank you very much.

Pillover asked politely that, for a graduation gift, his parents transfer the title of the townhouse in London into his name, which they did. This finally and forever separated Dimity from any further dependency upon their good will. He and his sister were not necessarily *estranged* from their evil genius parents so much as they were *mutually indifferent*.

Accordingly, Pillover continued to travel to London regularly, sometimes seeing Agatha and sometimes not. She continued to treat him with a mild sisterly affection, which he learned to accept as his due. They did have what amounted to a friendship. This was rare enough between members of the opposite sex (especially gentleman academics and lady spies) for Pillover to value it for its own sake. He only *most of the time* wished it were something more significant.

∼

March 1867 ~ The least select parlor in all of London

It's possible that things would have continued between them in this manner for the rest of their lives. Agatha was certainly content with their relationship, when she thought about it at all. She valued Pillover for his unchanging nature and steady countenance. She could always depend upon Pillover to be *Pillover*, to say Pilloverian things, sometimes in Latin, and do Pillover actions, generally in a slightly depressive manner. She would have forced herself to think of him as nothing more than her good friend's decent younger brother, also a friend himself now, but not particularly key to her life except in the unchanging stability that he represented.

That's how things *might* have continued. And no doubt Pillover would've let them. He was not the kind of man to put himself forward, especially when that action might have held *her* back. Or that was how Agatha thought about it later, after she understood him better.

Lord Akeldama sent her on a mission. Nothing new in that. It was a relatively simple one and Agatha found it depressingly easy to execute. Nothing new there either. It all took place in London. It was a simple matter of retrieving some rather damning paperwork about a major dirigible accident and shoddy workmanship, all concerning a man with a familiar name: Buss.

Perhaps *retrieving* was the wrong term. The paperwork in question did not belong to either Agatha or her vampire employer. Technically, the term was *stealing*. Technically, this mission was also insulting, since Lord Akeldama had a ready supply of individuals far better suited to this kind of activity than she.

But he'd issued precise instructions on exactly what she was to look for and where. Consequently, she found it and took it and met with Lord Akeldama, and would have given it to him and thought no more on the subject except that her assignment didn't end there. Sometime later he called her back, over the same paperwork.

"You are to take this to his daughter's house now. She is not in residence this evening, worry not. Simply place it upon her bed, like a lily pad upon a pond."

Agatha did not understand why he was bringing lily pads and ponds into the discussion. There was no need to slap her with unwarranted metaphors at this point in their association.

"What are you about, Lord Akeldama, distracting me with lily pads? Are you pitting intelligencers against one another?"

"So you remember who his daughter is?"

"Her name has changed many times over the years, but it has not been that long since we were all in finishing school together. I recognize the original, of course. Those papers are about Preshea Buss's father." Then Agatha thought about her own words. Almost ten years. Perhaps it had been a long time since finishing school.

"You read the papers, my wallflower?"

"Of course. I always read them."

He smiled at her, showing fang, an aggressive move and a threat. She did not care. He would never hurt her. She had made herself far too useful to bite.

"Why are you sending me into the house of Preshea Buss to leave behind a file containing the information that will destroy her own father?"

"Why not?" responded the vampire, which meant he didn't want her to know his reasoning.

Agatha did not care to ponder the machinations and manipulations of the deal he had likely made with Preshea. She was really asking why it had to be *her*, Agatha, doing this, and not one of his drones. Why did *she* have to go traipsing into her old enemy's house?

But Lord Akeldama wasn't going to tell her a single one of his reasons, even the one that pertained directly to her.

So Agatha went to Preshea Buss's house and did exactly as ordered, right down to how carefully and lightly she rested those papers on Preshea's bed.

She only ever saw that house that one time, but she remembered it forever. And much later she suspected that *that* was Lord Akeldama's design in sending her there.

It was a townhouse, but not at all like her own. This was a townhouse that had once been grand. Thirty years ago or more, it had been decorated to the very height of fashion. Now it felt abandoned, although it had clearly been cleaned and tended recently. It was not home. It had none of the friendly touches that Dimity put into their abode. It had no worn places on furniture where Pillover sat reading Cicero. No plush rug before a fire. No warm quilts or friendly, misshapen cushions.

What struck Agatha most was how cold the place felt. There were no personal touches anywhere, not even in Preshea's bedroom. It was very lonely. It was the house of someone who had shut herself away from the world, who had had marriages of intent but not love, who had no friends and no family. There was no doubt in Agatha's mind that Preshea would be using the paperwork now sitting on her bed to destroy her own father. Preshea was that kind of person.

Agatha left that unfriendly house feeling sad for a person whom she had never even liked. Feeling grateful that Dimity and Pillover had adopted her for no good reason. Because without them, she probably would have turned out exactly the same way.

Agatha thought about Preshea during the entire carriage ride back to her own small townhouse, where Pillover sat waiting for her, reading in front of a fire, for no other reason than that he liked her company and was in town for the weekend.

She settled in her usual spot staring at the flames, thinking about the past, thinking about her own personality. Wondering whether, if she'd been married multiple times by now with the intent to widow, her house would be unhappy. Wondering whether that was to be her fate regardless. She had no doubt that eventually Dimity would leave, for Dimity had never wanted to be an intelligencer. If Dimity found herself an obscure aristocrat to marry and retired to the countryside as she'd always wished, what would happen to this place? It was Pillover's, not hers. And he would no longer have a reason to come to London. He was not her actual brother and they could not meet like this in the eyes of society, not without Dimity around to act as buffer. Who then would Agatha come home to when she returned from her travels? Would she even need to return at all?

She thought about what Preshea had gained, if anything, from her life so far. And she thought about what she had gained, and compared them. Agatha considered all her experiences and travels and where they had taken her, and the great big gaps that were left in her humanity. She thought about the things she had consciously decided against, like marriage and children, and the begetting of both.

"Pill, please don't take this amiss, but you like me well enough, don't you?"

Pillover looked up, startled. It's possible he had not yet noticed her. After a pause, he said, "I would go so far as to say you are one of my favorite people."

"Because I am familiar?"

"Because you are you."

"A kind of adopted sister, I suppose."

"Is that not what you intended?"

"It's perfectly acceptable."

"Agatha, what has happened? You are not usually so

frank with me, nor so pensive about our relationship. Such as it is."

She turned to look at him. His face was beautiful in the firelight. He was all dark brows and angled cheeks, his somber expression planed by shadows.

"I saw my future tonight, or one possible version of it."

He pursed his lips. "Was it not what you expected?"

"It was exactly what I expected and that is making me think."

"Why?"

"It was lonely." She reached up to unpin her hair, feeling stretched by the tight knot holding it back. "When you go home to Oxford, is there anyone who waits for you, by the fire, the way you wait for me?"

"I rarely light a fire. I'm usually sidetracked by other things."

"That means no?"

"It does."

"Why do you do it here, then? For me, when you visit us in London?"

Pillover put his book aside and leaned back, looking up at the ceiling as if searching for inspiration, or enlightenment, or grace. "It's not out of brotherly devotion, I'll tell you that much."

Agatha paused at that statement. She thought about Pillover now and Pillover then, ten years ago. As a baby-faced boy seeking her out at parties on dirigibles. As a leggy adolescent insisting on a dance. As a beautiful, sullen adult, always trying to find her even when she wished to stay hidden. It could hardly be more than that, could it? That she was his sister's friend? That she was quieter than other girls? That she rarely demanded conversation. That she rarely flirted. That she never fell in love with him or chatted at him the way all the other silly girls did.

"If this is not sibling affection between us, then what is it?"

"Friendship," suggested Pillover. "Just plain old affection."

"Why?" she asked, genuinely curious. Thinking about him taking care of her when she was ill all those years ago. He had clearly felt obligated. Why else had he come up specially just to play nursemaid if not out of brotherly duty? Why else sit up late by a fire waiting for her? It was all very confusing.

Pillover shook his head as her, as if annoyed by her ignorance. Well, she *was* chattering at him and asking questions. It was not normal for them, and something he specifically abhorred, especially in women.

"Sorry." She dipped her head. "You don't have to answer."

"I like you, Agatha. I've always liked you. Does it need to be more or different than that?"

"Oh." She blinked at him. What a simple explanation. "I like you, too." The admission surprised her. But she did. She liked his quiet company and his stoic ways. She liked the way he looked and the way he looked at her. And for the very first time in her life, she was terrified of loneliness. She was almost thirty years old and she had seen more of the world than most, but she did not know the corner of it that was reserved for human contact. She didn't know the places of the human heart.

They liked each other. He had looked after her when she was sick, so obviously he was not repulsed by her body. Maybe he would be open, just this once, to a dalliance. And maybe she would not feel so lonely, if they did not part ways when the fire died down.

"Pillover," she said, girding her loins almost literally,

"Would you consider coming with me to—" She stopped herself.

"Where?"

She stood.

"But the fire is not out." He sounded plaintive, as though she was denying him by cutting short their evening together.

That decided her. "Would you like to spend the rest of the night in my bed? With me, I mean?"

"What? I say. I mean, *what*?" He almost shouted it.

Agatha giggled. "Don't wake your sister with your shock on this particular matter, Pillover, please."

"Are you ribbing me, Agatha? Because that's not on. Have a little care for a fellow's finer feelings."

"No, I assure you I'm quite serious."

"You *are* in a strange mood this evening."

Agatha would have felt disheartened except that he was looking up at her with eager eyes, and he hadn't run away at her shocking request.

"I've never done it, you see?"

"Slept in the same bed as someone?" His voice cracked a little.

"You know what I mean. We were taught seduction at finishing school, but I've never had to use those particular skills. Not my best lesson anyway."

"Please don't take this wrong, but I can tell."

Agatha giggled again. She was nervous, but also he was funny.

"What makes you want to do it now, with me?" he asked, and then added quickly, "I am not averse – quite the opposite – just confused."

She shook her head, not sure, only knowing that he felt safe, and he would not let her be alone, and he cared, and when he was in their house it was neither cold nor empty.

"Have you ever?" she asked.

He shook his head fast. "So don't expect much, but I'm willing to try."

"Are you really?" She was suddenly terrified and hopeful and oddly hot all at once. She turned to look at the fire to see if it had spiked for some reason, but it was actually burning low.

She held out her hand, and after a moment, he took it. His palm was smooth from a scholar's life, soft and sinewy thin. Hers was chubby but capable and callused in places no lady had calluses. She pulled him to standing, because she was strong enough, and led them from the friendly fire to her cold room.

Agatha wasn't sure what she expected from conjugal intimacy. She had read a little in books, and there had been some training. She might have asked Sophronia, but they didn't have that kind of friendship. Agatha didn't have that kind of personality either way. She guessed that relations between a man and a woman would be awkward, and messy, and painful. And it was all of those things. It was also sweet, and somehow beautiful – like he was.

What surprised her most was the sensation of full contact, skin against skin, and how much she adored it. Every touch she'd ever had with any human before had been separated by fabric. She didn't know until that moment that she resented gloves and layers of skirts. It turned out that the skin of another person was a necessary thing that prior to this night the whole world had conspired to deny her. This one man had broken a famine of flesh and made himself both exceptional and vital, because of the nothingness that had come before him.

Pillover was far more gentle than she had expected. He touched her lightly, with stuttering caution. His fingers jumped from one part of her body to the next, as if he were lighting a candelabra, and with each new caress he might be burned by the one that had come before.

While she knew that he had even less experience than she did in such matters, he had clearly studied a great deal more on the subject. She got the impression that he had committed certain passages to memory, and developed certain preferences of interest that guided his approach.

Their awkwardness became something to be solved through embarrassed whispered conversation. She was grateful for the dark. The messiness became something dealt with afterwards, as one might deal with any illness or injury, with soft warm cloths and medicinal efficiency. And Pillover had already aptly demonstrated an acumen for such things. The pain was fleeting, less significant than anything Agatha had felt in the field, so much so that she wondered that such a palaver was always made of it.

Afterwards, when they lay together as a tangled mess of naked limbs, she could not stop touching him for the wonder of being able to. He could not stop kissing her, possibly for the same reason. Kisses in odd places that were significant to him, and becoming so to her now, too.

He liked his lips against her fingers, particularly the crescent moon at the base of her thumbnail, as though he were recreating the worship of ancient goddesses crossing the sky, softly and with reverence. He had the same patience as those ancient people, to accept the capricious nature of her whimsy with grace. Even in this moment, their being together for one night, he had done only as she requested without concern for himself. Agatha thought it was weird how all the literature always spoke of it being the woman who gave, and the woman who lost, when it felt as if Pillover was the one at risk.

She didn't want to think about the fact that this was because he clearly wanted more of her. He wanted her to stay longer. He wanted something significant. While both of them knew that she did not. She was taking advantage of his good will and romantic nature, of his strange devotion over the years that had culminated in her moment of curiosity.

She ran her hands along his arms, so pale for never seeing the sun and lifting only books. Perhaps it was not her fault that she was leading him on. For he had known all along what kind of creature she was. Just as she knew how much he loved his forgotten Roman poetry. How loyal he was to his frivolous sister and her eccentric friends. How many times over the years he had been the one to come to her, to help them. She knew his nature, and she knew in some small way what she was doing to him, and that this was his heartbreak they risked. Because no matter how much she believed this was just curiosity and physical touch – his lips *were* always gentle and his gestures filled with yearning.

She knew what she was doing to him. And she knew it was cruel, but she also couldn't stop. Because to have something given so easily that turned out to be something she didn't know she'd been missing, was like traveling to a foreign land inside her own skin. The unfamiliar sensation of loving and being loved was too much like happiness, and even Agatha was not strong enough to let that go.

∼

Pillover was very careful with her. He would continue to be so for the few precious years that followed. Their patterns did not change significantly from what had come before. He still lived in Oxford and went up to London only occasionally, when Agatha was in town. He still teased his sister for her silly ways. Dimity still left them alone together in front of the fire.

If Dimity knew that those evenings more often than not culminated in Agatha's bed, she said nothing on the subject. Well, she wouldn't. If any of the staff noticed Pillover's bed was rarely slept in at the London house, they had been hired for their discretion.

Pillover and Agatha might have run into serious trouble, of course. There was even one horrible moment when Pillover actually wished for a child. As if he might tie Agatha to him with that. Which was an awful thing to think, because what would she do then? What would she become but miserable? Trapped by this experimental whimsy of hers into exactly the life she did not want. What would he do under those circumstances? Keep her in his shabby little cottage in Oxford as if she were a favorite book? On a tutor's salary, alone most of the day?

So he pushed the horror of that future and possibility aside, looked seriously into protective measures, and took them. And she did the same. Between them they learned to be quite experimental, and specifically careful, and no inconvenience resulted beyond the occasional giggle over an impossible position, wobbly legs, and maximum cleanup.

She was in town more frequently during that time. One conversation with her even gave him a clue as to why. It was an odd and out-of-character chat, which was probably why he remembered it so well. Apparently, her presence in London had to do with Sophronia, of all people. Pillover hadn't seen the Wicker Chicken in years – no doubt by design. Sophronia didn't hide the way Agatha, the Wallflower, did. But if Sophronia didn't want to be found, Pillover certainly wasn't the man to do so.

He and Agatha were talking quietly late one night, and

she mentioned that she was taking over a household assignment that had once belonged to Sophronia.

"That's odd, isn't it? I mean, you don't usually work the same commission. Aren't you, I don't know, opposing sides?" said Pillover.

Agatha giggled at him. "Sides? As if this were a game of cricket? I assure you there are no sides, but this one is a game changer."

"Oh?" He didn't pry, because usually she wouldn't tell him, but with this she seemed to think it necessary. As though she was protecting him with knowledge.

"London has an apex predator in its midst. Has done for a while now, but soon the predator will come of age."

"A new vampire queen?" That was all Pillover could think of that might cause such a stir in supernatural London. So great a stir that even Lord Akeldama seemed worried and had pulled his best asset out of the field. But wait – Agatha had said *come of age*.

"A child?" he asked.

"A preternatural."

Pillover had heard of them, of course, in a loose, intellectual way. He knew, for example, that preternaturals were the only things vampires and werewolves feared. But they were so rare he had never thought to meet one in his lifetime. Although, he supposed, he wasn't going to meet this one. But Agatha was.

"Are you taking over as governess or some other household staff?" He tried not to sound hopeful, because if so, that meant she would be staying in London for a long while. Longer than ever before.

"Oh no, just keeping an eye on the house in question until we can get proper staff installed. The butler is proving difficult to circumvent."

Pillover was surprised by her loquaciousness, but he

supposed this was technically someone else's assignment. "Sounds outside of your particular expertise."

"I did make that point at the time."

"You will be careful, though?" He worried at his lower lip with nervous teeth, then caught himself at it and stopped. "They are quite dangerous, are they not? Preternaturals?"

Agatha tilted her head and considered. "Not to me, I don't think. Only to supernatural creatures. Vampires fear them." She gave a tiny smile, as if this was pleasant to think about.

"Still, you *will* be careful?"

"I am always careful."

He knew she was, but that didn't stop the occasional bruises garnered in dark alleys. Bruises that he now got to see live and in person on her upper arms.

So Pillover, oddly, had reason to be grateful for the presence of a preternatural child and an obstreperous butler in London, as they afforded him a romantic dalliance of several years.

Pillover was young enough to hope it might last forever. He was naive enough to hope that it might parlay into something more, even with no child to bind her. He was careless enough to hope that she might commit some small part of herself to him beyond soft touches and long nights.

He returned to his cottage in Oxford and tried to make it cozy and warm, just in case she ever came to visit him. She never did, but it was not a bad little house, and eventually he kept it tidy and homey for its own sake. Maybe he stayed up too late in his study by the fire translating something or other because his bed was empty, or maybe it was just that his study was now welcoming and comfortable.

Pillover had colleagues who shared his interests, if nothing else, and eventually he invited one of them for tea.

Sorrinson Fausse-Maigre was a junior tutor like himself, and he liked Pillover's walnut wood-paneled rooms with the warm, buttery cream curtains and the sage wallpaper. He liked the books everywhere and declared that they should "meet regularly with some of the other like-minded chaps." And, as if by magic, on Wednesday nights Pillover found himself hosting a kind of book club (which he would *never* call a secret society, but which basically was). On Wednesdays they argued vociferously about the latest trends in linguistics, or lost Germanic declensions, or some obscure point of the intersection between pictographic language and syllabic ones and philosophical thought. It wasn't so bad, actually. And Pillover wasn't so alone.

He did learn that he had to be careful about letting his two worlds collide. He and Agatha often talked about his work, mostly because they couldn't talk about hers. At one point he was having a particularly difficult time with the editor of an academic press who kept challenging his verb choices. It was frustrating to have to explain his decisions in every editorial letter, especially when he knew he was in the right. This was Latin, after all. Agatha made sympathetic murmurs and agreed with him that the editor was *clearly* an idiot.

It had just been one of many little conversations, kissing the fingers of her hand and whinging on about this editor. He hadn't thought more about it.

But over the next month, that particular editor was revealed to have published three manuscripts of a deceased scholar without consulting any relations, and *also* not crediting the work properly. Then, when that only resulted in a demotion, it was made known through mysterious sources that the same editor had also had a dalliance with said dead scholar's wife, possibly when the scholar was not yet dead.

Pillover couldn't be certain Agatha was behind the character defamation, but he *was* certain that he couldn't ask. He didn't want to give her the idea that she *should* be behind such a thing, or undertake similar activities on his behalf. But he was pretty confident that it was all her doing.

He continued his association with the Order of the Brass Octopus. He reported to her anything of interest, as he assumed that was what he was there to do. The Roman vampire medical texts came few and far between now. He assumed he had translated the bulk of Lord Akeldama's collection. But that is the thing about secret societies – once you're in, it takes a lot to get you out. Sometimes Pillover thought the OBO had forgotten he was there, but he always attended any obligatory Oxford event, even if he rarely said anything. He had become a fixture, even though he contributed little to the society or conversation.

He still wasn't certain why he was there. The OBO never seemed to be involved in anything particularly nefarious, just science. Lots and lots of science. Inventions, too. More Vieve's thing, he always thought. But they might, he supposed, cross into Lord Akeldama's territory and therefore Agatha's at some point. If she wanted him inside, he would stay inside, even if he did feel a lot like an interloping classicist.

The Wednesday book club got its own interloping scientist – a geologist friend of Sorrinson's, name of Fellburt, fell in with them. He was of a sunny disposition, concerned with measuring things accurately. "For scale," he always said. He reminded Pillover a little bit of his sister. Which ordinarily wouldn't have recommended the fellow, but he saw so little of Dimity these days he rather missed her.

So Fellburt came on Wednesdays to Pillover's cottage, and did his best to argue the nuances of languages from an outsider's perspective. This turned out to be pleasingly novel and only added to the discourse.

It was Fellburt who brought Pillover a large and beautiful rock that had been sliced in half to show off stunning striations of brown and gold. Fellburt claimed it would make an excellent bookend and that it matched Pillover's decorative style.

This startled Pillover who, first of all, hadn't known that he had a *decorative style* and secondly, had never had anyone bring him a gift merely for the sake of it before, simply because they thought he might like it. He was very flattered and thanked Fellburt effusively.

"Old chap, think nothing of it. We geologists have spectacular rocks just lying about everywhere, all willy-nilly."

"Do you indeed?"

"Comes with the territory."

"And what's this one called?"

"Oh, didn't I say? That's an *agate*."

Pillover was so taken with his new rock, and the complexity of its colors, and the similarities in their names that he said, rather injudiciously, "Reminds me of someone."

Fellburt looked at him sharply. "You have a *someone*, do you?"

Pillover shook his head. "Merely an old friend."

"Ah, well then, may we all be so lucky as to have such *friends*." Fellburt was damned perceptive, for a geologist. He added, with a rummy look on his face, "There are many types of agates, did you know? Should you like one for your friend, I could find you another."

Pillover thought he would like one for Agatha. "Do they come with even more red to them?"

"Indeed they do." Fellburt cocked his head and twinkled thoughtfully at Pillover.

"No rush," said Pillover.

By the time Agatha was back in town and Pillover was to visit her again, he was in possession of a piece of carnelian agate that fit in the palm of his hand and was almost the color of her hair, at least in parts.

She took it from him with one of her softer, sweeter, more private smiles. "It's lovely, Pill, thank you."

"Can I call you Agate?" he asked. Careful, worried it might be an insult, but wanting something special and private between them that was only his, even if it was just a name.

She turned the smile on him. "Please do. I've never really liked Agatha. I've always counted myself fortunate that I tend to go by a different name, a secret coded one, or nothing at all."

She could also, he knew, learn to respond to a new name quickly, because that too was part of her training.

So he called her Agate after that, testing it out around the fire, while she petted the stone that he had gifted her. And later, breathing it out against the hair that was the color of that stone. And later still in letters, the occasional ones that he wrote addressed to the townhouse where he knew she wasn't, but which he hoped she enjoyed coming home to when he could not be there in person. His words and that stone waited for her, even when he himself could not.

CHAPTER NINE
THE LANGUAGE OF LOSS

March 1869 ~ The least select parlor in all of London

Agatha thought things were going rather well, not that they were *going* anywhere, but the status quo was pleasing. There was no future to discuss, so none was talked of, and she and Pillover spent what little time they had together pleasantly. She supposed the ignorant might call such a thing *a grand affaire*, although it felt not so much *grand* as small and inconsequential, if sweetly special in its way. It was minor, and of little significance to anyone except perhaps the two of them. She even had a nickname that only he used, which she liked overmuch, because it fit so well with her life. After all, she had many names – one for when she visited Vieve in Paris; and another for when she pretended to be the owner of Lord Akeldama's estate in Italy; and another when she was the sketch artist attached to an archaeological excavation in Egypt; and another for when she was the grieving widow following up on her husband's investments in the Boston railroad. Many names.

But Agate was her favorite. It was the one least used, and only by one person. Which made it special.

Sometimes, although increasing rarely over the years, she even had to use the name Miss Woosmoss. The spring of 1869 was one of those times.

She was back in London, not because of an assignment, or a liaison with Lord Akeldama, but because of something unexpected. Not to say *inconvenient*. It was something connected to her past life that some less acute person might call her *real life* – not that it had ever felt very *real*. Miss Woosmoss's father had died, and Agatha returned home to deal with it.

She hadn't spoken to her late father in years. They had nothing in common and so no conversation could result, not that either of them were naturally loquacious to start with. He had dismissed her as useless in infancy and she had never done anything to disabuse him of the notion. She doubted that he ever once wondered what she'd been doing all these years. How she'd managed to survive. Why she had not married. Things that might concern even the most absentminded of fathers over a daughter had never troubled Mr Woosmoss over Miss Woosmoss. Agatha had no idea what *had* troubled her father, but it'd certainly never been her.

Lord Akeldama informed Agatha by coded post that Mr Woosmoss had shuffled off the mortal coil. The vampire left the conversion of this information into action entirely up to her. Agatha decided that she had better return home. She was her father's only heir – unless what little he had was entailed to a distant male relation she knew nothing about, but that only happened in silly novels. She was required to handle the paperwork, if nothing else.

For once, Pillover was not in London when she arrived. He usually had a mysterious ability to determine when she was back in town, no doubt based on the nature and frequency of her letters to him.

Dimity was also not in residence. She had not even left an indication as to where she might be. Which meant she was no doubt on assignment somewhere dangerous.

For many years, Dimity had been working for either the War Office or the Home Office, Agatha wasn't certain which. It wasn't done to inquire too closely. Dimity, for her part, probably knew that Agatha continued her indenture to Lord Akeldama. Dimity also knew how much Agatha enjoyed traveling, and how unexpected a luxury it was for a lady, even an intelligencer, to be indulged by her patron in going abroad. It had taken Agatha well over a decade to train Lord Akeldama into reliance on, and acceptance of, her usefulness as a mobile asset, not to mention the many languages she now spoke. They both knew she wasn't going to switch patrons and train a new one into accepting her wanderlust eccentricities from the ground up.

Perhaps Agatha was a little underpaid and overused because of this, but she had renewed her indenture with Lord Akeldama twice now, and she expected to do so again.

Dimity, on the other hand, Agatha would have thought married by now, leaving the game to those more eager to play it. Dimity had always said being an intelligencer was for special occasions and what she really wanted was a normal life – whatever that meant. But they were both over thirty now, and Dimity was still not married.

It was possible that Dimity's training and her dabbling in and out of government and politics with powerful men of flexible moral fiber had given her a jaded opinion of the male sex. Or it was possible, through near constant exposure to the species, that she had become too picky. Either way, Dimity was now firmly on the shelf. Agatha thought it unlikely her friend would settle down at this point. It was getting too late. Unless, of course, she and Sophronia interfered to arrange matters on their friend's behalf.

She thought to ask Pillover about it, but the townhouse was entirely empty – cold and shut up, as if both Plumleigh-Teignmotts had been away for quite some time.

So Agatha dealt with her father's effects (there were few) and his estate (in debt and mostly sold off). With the help of one of Lord Akeldama's business-minded drones and no small expense, she saw everything settled to her satisfaction, if not to her father's or his creditors'. Who cared for either of those parties? The one was dead and the other could never find her again, should she wish it.

Afterwards she was, for the first time in more than twenty years, rather at a loss for what to do with herself. Lord Akeldama had sent someone else to deal with the problem in Prague that she hadn't been able to satisfactorily conclude. The vampire had nothing else for her just yet. He had told her to rest and relax, of all things, and take the opportunity to *enjoy the delights* of London for a change.

This Agatha did not know how to do. She had no means of entertainment or relaxation without Pillover around to read her Latin and warm her bed.

Which begged the question, when had he become a necessary part of her existence?

She went to some museums and galleries, even tried the opera and the symphony – all at Lord Akeldama's insistence and expense. It turned out that she enjoyed none of these things when she had no mark to track, no object to steal, and no information to extract. She had little appreciation for art that was not her own special brand of magician's sleight of hand.

She read some books, but preferred the newspaper, because at least she had an outside chance of influencing politics through some means or other. She would curl up on the rug in front of the fire and pore over the evening paper, looking for hidden messages or covert signs of the machinations of foreign governments.

The death of her father, a man whom she had worked so hard to ensure would leave little impact on herself, had somehow left her feeling unmoored and adrift. She realized that she had been skulking for so long, she'd traded her whole life on being forgotten. She had awakened in a small cell in a land where she did not speak the language holding a letter from a vampire with the certain knowledge that one of the few people who remembered her existence was now dead. At some point, if no one remembered her, was she, in fact, no one? A wraith of information and nothing more. Not even a whole person. And so she found herself feeling lonely, stuck in the house where, up until now, she was generally afforded the company of friends and even a lover. It was disconcerting, to say the least.

As a result, she was feeling a little sorry for herself, alone by the fire eating a bought hand pie with an inferior hot-water crust, when a clatter at the door heralded the return of somebody. Probably Pillover, since Dimity was, by training, rather quieter upon entering a house, even her own.

~

Pillover made his way through the townhouse, following the feeling of fireplace warmth and the smell of food. Someone was home and he knew for certain that it wasn't Dimity. He'd just left his sister in starry-eyed bliss over a large man with a propensity for pirouettes and a strangely deadly manner, who had asked Pillover for permission to marry his impossible sister. As if Pillover held any sway over Dimity. Even if he did, he should never presume to choose for her a husband when he didn't even understand her taste in evening slippers.

Dimity had been fixing a broken vampire hive and had called him up to help, not because she wished his opinion of Sir Crispin Bontwee (the pirouetting chappy), but because she was throwing an intellectual salon and required the presence of a noted Oxford intellectual of repute to add consequence to the gathering. Pillover was only a junior don of very little consequence, but tell that to Dimity.

He'd taken Sorrinson along with him. Sorrinson was more properly known as Professor Fausse-Maigre and had recently written a philosophical diatribe in the guise of a popular guidebook towards elevated thought called *The Higher Common Sense*. Much to everyone's shock, it had proven startlingly successful with the masses. It made Sorrinson a desirable presenter at intellectual salons, and while the man was by nature rather shy and retiring, he gave an excellent waffle in front of a crowd of dilettantes. The society matrons in particular adored him. He was, in fact, an excellent orator and a decent teacher, which in academic circles was far more the exception than the rule.

The salon having been a resounding success, the vampire hive apparently saved by his sister, and said sister deposited in the surprisingly willing arms of Sir Crispin, Pillover and Sorrinson had returned to London.

They'd parted ways at the station, Sorrinson to his club and Pillover to his townhouse, with apologies at there being no spare bed. There was a spare bed. In fact, because Dimity was still up north with her knight, and Pillover rarely slept in his assigned one, there were two spare beds. But on the off chance that Agatha was in town, Pillover didn't want anyone, certainly not Sorrinson Fausse-Maigre, intruding on what little time they had together.

To Pillover's delight, Agatha was sitting in her usual

place in front of the fire. She had changed for the evening into a night-rail. Her hair was long and loose and wavy from being braided.

She was clearly in a pensive mood. Something dark had happened recently. Pillover had learned, over the years, that she got this way when she'd had to do something on assignment that she didn't like. Or didn't believe in. She was always in the worst moods when someone had died. He never asked if she had done the killing, because he really did not want to know. He'd rather think it *might* be her fault, than to have it absolutely confirmed. Assuming she would tell him the truth, of course, which was unlikely. Best just not to ask.

Regardless, Agatha was definitely in one of those moods. Truth be told, Pillover was unsettled, too. Surprised by seeing his sister smitten. Seeing Dimity, for lack of a more poetic way of putting it, *in love*. Really in love, with an upstanding minor knight of fine physique and sportsman-like sensibilities. Dimity had gone and gotten herself fatally attached to one of the Corinthian types who had made Pillover's life a living hell as a schoolboy at Bunson's. The kind of man who enjoyed hunting and a snifter of brandy after dinner. Who kept hounds, for goodness sake. Not that Pillover necessarily disliked Sir Crispin in particular, but still, he was unsettled. And now here was Agatha, which delighted him no end, but who was also unsettled.

Pillover wanted to ask her what had happened. But of course he couldn't. Instead, he settled in his wingback chair. Unlike her, he couldn't move quietly enough for her not to notice.

She watched him. "It's good to see you home."

He acknowledged the small chink in her armor with information, because he knew she valued it highly. "I was up north visiting Dimity. She was completing an infiltration and repair. Needed my help, or the help of a professorial type. I took my friend Sorrinson along."

"And were you successful?"

"Very. I have some distressing news, however."

"Do you indeed?"

"I believe my sister will be leaving us."

"Oh? Where is she going? A trip?"

"Ah no, something a bit more permanent."

"She is moving out of London?" Agatha was justifiably surprised. Dimity lived and breathed London society – it was one of her main passions. "Surely not. An assignment is taking her somewhere for an extended period of time?"

"More like a change of status."

"My dear Pill, are you being coy with me? That's not your style."

"Apologies, Agate, no. I believe she has finally found the man she wishes to marry. A knight, of all things – Sir Crispin Bontwee."

"Ah." Agatha looked sad. "This will impact our arrangement and this house."

"Why?"

"I cannot be seen to stay here alone without my female friend. Not when it is your house and you come and stay here regularly yourself."

"Why not? When you are so rarely seen at all?"

"It is not *my* reputation I worry for, Pillover. It is yours. You come to town to visit your sister. If your sister is not in town, then you can have no easy excuse to visit the place. You cannot pursue an academic career at an august institution of higher learning and be seen to keep and visit a mistress. And there could be no other explanation for such behavior. It is simply too much moral turpitude in anyone, especially an Oxford don. You're neither an aristocrat nor a werewolf."

Pillover understood at last the depths of his sister's betrayal. In pursuing her own dream of romance and happiness, she had inadvertently destroyed the small bit that he had managed to carve out for himself.

Agatha was right. Dimity's marriage to the man of her dreams would put an end to their affaire. It actually, physically hurt him to think about it. Because for all he loved his Latin translations, and tolerated his students, and fussed over his lesson plans, Pillover only looked forward to his few trips up to London. He lived for Agatha's red hair spread out over the faded pillowcase. For the little smile he got when he kissed her fingertips, one after another. For the silken warmth of her soft skin. For the moments when she was safe in his arms and he did not have to fight to suppress the sinking sensation of her being out in the world, alone, and in danger. Out where she depended upon the fact that she was invisible – when for him, when she was there, she was all he could see. How could he bear it, to know she was out there fighting and never coming back to him? Not even briefly.

"Where will you go when you are home?" he asked, trying to keep the hurt out of his voice.

"The world has changed enough for me to find a boarding house that caters to ladies of decent reputation. Or Lord Akeldama can find some maiden aunt or other in need of companionship. It is not so hard. There are always lonely and forgotten women in this city." She said it as if she were one of them now.

He wanted to say how much he would miss her. Explain that she was never alone except that she chose to be. But he didn't.

She said, "Is it possible to turn into a ghost without dying? I think sometimes I'm already there."

"I see you." He rose to pop another log onto the fire. It

was unlikely they would be going to bed anytime soon if she was waxing philosophical. "I've always seen you."

"Yes, I know. I find that remarkable."

"Don't be silly." He resumed the wingback chair, crossed his hands over his lap, tilted his head at her. Trying for casual but intent on making his point. "The rest of them do, too – my sister, Sophronia, Sidheag, even Vieve. I know you never talk about it, but I know you see them, too, probably more regularly than you ought."

"Sid has her pack. Sophronia has her important work. Vieve has her gadgets and her heartaches. And you tell me that now Dimity has found herself Sir Crispin. I'm not relevant anymore. Not to them."

"You're relevant to me." He shook his head at her and tutted, trying to lighten the mood. "Don't be maudlin, that's my job."

"It's just— What do I have but other people's secrets?"

"Me," said Pillover promptly, feeling brave, encouraged by this strange new facet of her personality that he'd never seen before. She was in an odd mood to admit weakness, or if not weakness, at least longing. He didn't think Agatha got lonely, if that's indeed what this was. "You have me."

She twitched a tiny smile at him. He sighed and crouched next to her on the rug, looking at her up close and intimate. "You never want to get serious about these matters. I've always understood that you realize what I want from you. We avoid the topic because you cannot bear to disappoint me."

She put a hand to his face. "You're meant to have a normal life. A nice wife keeping a lovely home for you, with a musty study full of books that she's not allowed inside. You're meant to have awkward children who read too much and care about mundane things. You were never meant to be mine."

He closed his eyes and tilted his face into her hand and let himself ache for the reality he'd never spoken of. Let himself absorb the fact that she had indeed known all along. That she had been denying them both from the start.

There were the calluses on the hand that cupped his face, calluses proper ladies didn't have – from drawstrings and knives, lock picks and chisels, weapons and tools he could not name and did not want to think about. He let himself enjoy the caress for as long he dared, then he stood and resumed his seat. "It seems neither of us has much of a choice in this matter."

Suddenly, desperately, Pillover wanted to press his face into the curve of her neck. He wanted to tip her over before the fire and nuzzle into the valley of her breasts, the juncture of her thighs, and the soft swell of her stomach. He had no idea why, he just yearned fiercely for the reassurance of her warmth. Her strong, rough hands would slide over his skin. She would trace words into his shoulder in all the living languages that he did not speak. And he would try to sink into her in every way he could before she disappeared again.

Strangely, it reminded him of his youth, away at school for the first time, when he would bury himself under the blankets, pull them high over his head and think of small comforts instead of large bruises.

Instead, he slumped back, let the quiet seep into his bones like the warmth of the flames.

Eventually, he just said what he was afraid of, because the thickness of the worry was becoming painful. "I'm scared that without me, you'll have no safe place anymore, Agate."

She looked back at him. "That I will lose all connection to what is decent and good?"

"Never would I dignify myself with such qualities. Just unmoored. Lost."

"I worry, too, especially now since my father has died."

Pillover twitched. He hadn't known that. Why hadn't he known? To be fair, he hadn't known that she had a father at all, although he supposed even Agatha must have come from somewhere.

She continued, "Not that he counted for much. But he did know who I was and that I existed. Without you and us and these moments by the fire will I get lost, and become unseen by everyone? Is there a part of me that wants that?"

He screwed his courage hard to the sticking point and said the thing he was certain she would never forgive him for. "There is one way we could keep these moments and this house. One way to stay together without issue."

She looked down.

"You could marry me." He would find some job in London, something suitably academic and dusty, perhaps with the Royal Society or one of the museums. He would suffer the aggravation of too much locomotion and too many people and living in a city he did not like for those times when she was home and she was his. Because she was worth that.

"No, Pill dear," she said, breaking up the dream that wasn't really one, because he could not see himself happy here either, not permanently, even if it were with her.

"But why?"

"Because you would want me to stay, as a wife should."

"And what's wrong with that?"

"Nothing at all, for a woman other than me. Pillover darling, have you learned nothing about me in all these years?"

"I know you are compelled to stay in motion. I know you worked to escape this place, and not just London, but all of England. I know you come back under sufferance. I know you love some of us, and some of this, but you refuse to stay too long. I do not know what motivates you. I've never understood why."

She picked up a glass of claret resting nearby and stared at the liquid. She never drank much. None of them did. Geraldine's girls did not lose control for any reason. They did not sacrifice their social power for alcohol, or anger, or love.

She took a tiny sip, merely wet her lips, then spoke, forming the words with great care. As if she had been thinking these thoughts for a long time, waiting for someone – for him – to ask.

"There is an art to always being a stranger. There is peace in being alone in a foreign land, where a language I do not speak becomes an ocean of calm in which I can safely swim. I can't explain it to you, Pill. How do I tell someone like you of the joy that comes from being adrift? You are so very settled. I sometimes think you started out that way."

Pillover looked at his right hand, inkstained, with the callus on the longest finger where his stylus rested. "I cannot deny it. I have always wanted to stay where it is safe and cozy."

She nodded. Sad, but not with him. "Whereas I feel if I stopped moving I might die, just fade away. I not only dwell in the shadows, it is my very lifeblood to keep chasing them."

"Why do you love traveling so much?" he asked. *Why do you love it more than me?*

"Because there is no other way to smell a place but to go there. There is no other way to see the light or feel the breeze, but to turn your face into it. There is no other moment in time but the country in which I find myself.

How do I know I exist if my surroundings never change? To be somewhere new, to go somewhere else, is the only way I can know myself as real."

"You like it?"

"Like what?"

"Being lost."

"I love it." She stood, abruptly. "Come to bed now, Pill, so I can get lost in you."

So he rose and held out his hand. They went to her cold little room like that – hand in hand and worlds apart. Where they could get lost in the familiarity of each other, one final time.

CHAPTER TEN
WEDDING SEASON

June 1870 ~ A decidedly select wedding with all the right people and some of the wrong ones

From the private record-keeping archives of DISTLA (drones in service to Lord Akeldama)

They saw each other again a year or so later, at the highly fashionable and remarkably well-attended wedding of one Miss Dimity Plumleigh-Teignmott to one Sir Crispin Bontwee.

The wedding was regarded by those who cared for such things as a touch scandalous. Sir Crispin was widely considered a *catch,* while Miss Plumleigh-Teignmott was a confirmed spinster of dubious taste and consequence and known to be *over thirty* years of age! The lady was walked down the aisle by her *brother*, one of the gentleman's groomsmen was an actual *werewolf*, and there were fully eight different kinds of cake.

Of course, anyone who was anybody and quite a few nobodies were in attendance, because what better spice is there for a wedding but scandal?

And eight forms of cake.

One of those nobodies was the bride's friend Miss Woosmoss, also a spinster, to whom age had not been so kind. When thought of at all, said friend was considered plain and retiring, and no one at the wedding danced with her except for those obligated by long association. The bride's brother, for example, was seen to do his gentlemanly duty, as was the bride's new husband, and a certain number of kilted werewolves who, for some reason, were attending *en masse* from some dubious place in Scotland called Castle Kingair.

All in all, the wedding was thought a great triumph of age over adversity and no one gave the union much prospective longevity. A flawed assessment, as the conjugal affiliation turned out to be wildly successful, shockingly fruitful, and relentlessly politically profitable. Sir Crispin had apparently undertaken the highly eccentric pastime of loving his wife, proving himself unreservedly happy in his choice – something society and the papers thought of as rather rude, not to say crass, but which suited him well enough when all was said and done. His wife, whom most would have been tempted to call *desperate* under the circumstances, also apparently having married out of actual affection for the sorry blighter, bolstered him over the years not only with children, but also and perhaps more important, with a certain flow of information that saw his consequence and standing improve with a steadiness that must, perforce, be attributed to skill and not luck. Theirs became one of the most desirable dinner invitations when Parliament was in session, and one of the most coveted house party invitations when it was not. The marriage was, in the end, by all standards of evaluation a resounding success.

Which was deeply annoying, honestly.

～

Pillover was aware, despite himself, that his sister's lace-trimmed wedding gown contained a full sixteen yards of satin in the skirt alone. It was a vision of swags and ruffles and three vertical rows of twelve satin bows each up the front and sides, with a lace train held in place by even more bows. He kept his sanity by counting them during the ceremony.

Dimity was a *vision*. Pillover wasn't entirely certain what *kind* of vision, but she was a vision of something... possibly a half-inflated dirigible. He was not alone in this feeling. Many of the attendees felt compelled to tell him how very well his sister looked (as if he cared).

He only got to dance with Agatha twice. Any more would have been overly attentive and therefore noteworthy. They hadn't seen each other in a year and he had to prevent his hand on her waist from clutching too hard, and his arms from pulling her too close.

There was only one moment from that wedding that stuck in his mind. It had stuck because it was one of those rare times when he had been watching Agatha unnoticed, for a change. She wasn't hiding. She was dancing, and she was dancing with a stranger whom Pillover couldn't identify as belonging to any of the manifold parts of his sister's life.

What he remembered was seeing Agatha's foot stepped on by the man. How he had to dampen the resulting weird instinct to cut her out and sit her down and check for bruises because she was limping. He stopped himself, of course – her welfare was not his concern – but he still made his way over after she'd resumed her chair. He pretended to look at a painting just above her head.

To any outside observer he appeared to be engaged in discourse with a nearby potted plant about the painting. Because Agatha was doing that thing where she was there-but-not-there, which meant that no one saw her.

"Is your foot all right, Agate?"

"Of course."

"Ah, it was intentional?"

"He's wearing very soft shoes."

"That's significant?"

"Those are not evening shoes. Those are more complicated. I think perhaps... climbing."

"Ah. Our friend was not invited?"

"Let me merely suggest that he did not come in through the front door. I'm thinking — Ah yes, there..."

Pillover turned to see whatever she was on about, but of course her attention was already refocused on the dancers.

"Lady Yaxton is down an emerald bracelet."

"Ah." Pillover nodded at the painting. "Jewel thief."

"Indeed. Your sister's preference in adornment and increase in consequence is widely known."

Pillover snorted. He did not pay attention to anything much with regard to fashionable trends, but even he knew a bride did not wear expensive jewelry on her wedding day, certainly not of the overabundant, sparkly kind that Dimity usually preferred. In fact, his sister was wearing nothing more extravagant than some opal earrings and an opal ring. The ring he knew without question was designed to deliver poison, but the set was not particularly valuable. The poison was just a precaution, and if the thief weren't careful, it would be used on him. Dimity had strong feelings about the sanctity of weddings.

Agatha followed his line of thought. "Quite so. And what kind of thief doesn't know what is worn or *not* worn on an occasion like today?"

"A foreign one. Or one who is not here for jewels alone."

"Opportunistic emeralds, you think?" Agatha tapped her chin with her fan, looking as though she had not considered that option.

"Will you be doing anything about him?" Pillover wondered.

"Not my concern, really. Why should I dampen his fun?"

"You're an odd duck, my Agate."

"Shove off, Pill. Some of us have real work to do."

He didn't ask what her work entailed at his sister's wedding. He was only grateful that they had fallen so easily into their old pattern, where they were friends of a kind, trading comforting barbs and minimal information at a ball. It spoke well of their future encounters. When they eventually happened.

It spoke ill of their dalliance. That she had so easily and freely thrown him over for their past selves. As if their being lovers were some small lapse in judgment, a brief dabbling in weak fantasy. A novel picked up and read and finished and that, in the end, had no impact on their real lives. For two whole years he had been hers as completely as any man ever could, and just like that, those years were dust motes and yearning.

He wondered if it had been worth it. If he might be worse off now for knowing exactly what he was missing.

He turned away and went to congratulate his sister.

He found her by the punch bowl experiencing a brief lull in well-wishers and sycophants.

AMBUSH OR ADORE

"Dance, old thing?" he asked. They were family, after all. It should carry some privilege.

"Why not, you blighter?"

He twirled her around sedately, as befitted her new station in life. She was a matron now, wouldn't do to be careless with a married woman.

"You look pretty tonight, Dim." He wasn't going to skimp on complimenting his own sister on her wedding day, even if it was Dimity.

"Have you ever thought about it, Pill?"

"Marriage? No, not really."

"Why not? We had a good example. I mean, our parents were evil and possibly quite mad, but they loved each other until the explosive end."

Pillover shook his head. "Oh no, it's not that. It's just that it wouldn't be fair."

"Fair to whom?"

"Whomever I married. My heart wouldn't be in it, you see. I already gave it away." He spun her around, trying to distract her, feeling awkward about having such a genuine conversation with his sister. But also feeling fragile from what had just happened with Agatha. He felt thin and worn and stretched, as though he were a bit of rubber bracing, overused and no longer quite so tough as it had once been.

Surprisingly, Dimity answered him in kind. "You can't keep waiting for her, Pill."

"Oh. That's not it, Dim. I'm not really waiting. Not anymore. It's just there's no point in trying with anyone else. When I gave my heart away, I gave the whole thing. I didn't hold any of it in reserve. Terribly careless, I know, but there it is."

"Oh Pill, you silly old thing."

"Habit is a rum deal when it takes over the emotions. Not that I pretend to sentimentality. But you know me. I've always liked things a certain way. Creature of habit, that's what, even in matters such as this."

"It's too bad, Pill. Really it is."

Pillover shook his head and grinned at her, hard, narrowed his eyes to keep back the burning. "I'll muddle through. That, too, is habit. You'll be happy though, won't you? It'd be a very good thing if you were and I should like it very much."

"I shall do my best."

"I recommend making it a habit."

"You should know."

Pillover went home alone to their townhouse (only not *theirs* anymore). The wedding was long over and his sister was safely afloat on a dirigible for Greece in fine style and with far too many trunks. And because there was no one there to stop him and no fire in the grate to pull him into the parlor, he climbed into Agatha's old bed and buried himself in stale blankets up to his nose. Then pulled them up and over his head for comfort.

The townhouse went up for sale the next day, and Pillover returned to Oxford.

∽

Winter 1873 ~ The newly opened Hypocras Club, London

Pillover wasn't sure about this new club. He was billeted in one of the upper floors and there seemed to be a great deal of late-night activity going on lower down. But he needed a place to stay in London. He'd long since sold the townhouse and his regular club was overfull due to the Royal Society's inconvenient hosting of an international assembly of entomologists. He was glad not to be staying there – bug people were excessively annoying. Well, to be fair, most scientists were annoying to classicists like him, but the bug people were really very tiresome.

He was still at a gentlemen's club for scientists, philosophers, and worthy intellectuals, but it was one that had some kind of loose association with the Order of the Brass Octopus. Since he was still an OBO member in good standing, the Oxford chapter had put in a good word for him and now here he was, staying in a strange club and trying not to be disturbed by how disturbing the place was.

At least there were no entomologists about. One had to be grateful for small mercies.

He was in town to meet with an old friend who had written to say she was coming from Paris for a presentation at the Royal Society on ghost preservation tanks, and did he have some time to spend the day with her looking at property? Honestly, what was the Royal Society about being so embarrassingly *active* of late? Truth be told, Pillover could hardly think of anything he would like to do less than visit London right now, but Vieve was also a friend of Agatha's. This was an opportunity to hear something about her, or barring that, at least to talk about her a little.

Agatha still sent him letters from foreign lands, of course, because Agatha always kept her promises. But they were sparse and sparsely written, merely proofs of the places she had been and that she was still alive. Which he was grateful to know, but they didn't really satisfy. She always signed them *Agate*. He loved that, even though he knew it was a practical choice. It was the perfect code name, one that literally only he knew meant it was her.

His old friend Vieve was back to being a woman again. Or, to be precise on the matter, she was no longer disguised entirely as a man. She had never given over masculine dress, it was only that now there were no fake mustaches, binding bandages, or simulated voice cracks. Their school years had been hard on both of them, he for the actuality of adolescence and she for the imitation of it. But now, in middling years, they were both comfortable with their respective outward appearances.

Vieve looked well enough for someone who had, not too long ago, had her heart well and truly broken and then in a fit of French passion unleashed an octopus automaton on Paris with disastrous results. He frowned. Then again, maybe that *had* been a long time ago. Still, a many-faceted individual, his friend Vieve. Very ardent about many things. Very French.

They met at a fashionable gentlemen's coffee house, where they drank indifferent beverages, smoked small cigars, and ruminated about their school days. Vieve announced she was in the market for a London retail establishment because she intended to dabble in trade and Pillover was gratifyingly appalled. Her eyes twinkled in delight at his evident shock. He lost it sooner than she liked because he remembered that Vieve was the very definition of eccentric inventor and he supposed not everyone had an independent income.

Fortified by Chelsea buns and curiosity, they trotted around town with an earnest young gentleman who knew a great many things about retail concerns. Pillover tried desperately to avoid paying any kind of attention – it was all so very ungentlemanly.

"So you genuinely intend to move *to London*, do you, and open a—" He paused, swallowed his disapproval. "*—hat* shop?"

Vieve knew exactly what he was doing. "I know, old chap, so very beneath your notice. You'll have to patronize it anyway, you understand? I shall need all the customers I can get at first, especially of your caliber."

Pillover hadn't any caliber to speak of and would have objected most strenuously, except that she was distracted by the fact that the latest property appeared to have a secret passageway of some kind.

"You haven't changed at all," he accused. "Secret passageway indeed. I suppose you're going to excavate a ruddy great cave for all your crafty devices and wicked ways, like a true evil genius?"

Vieve wiggled her eyebrows at him. "You can take the genius out of the secret passageway, but you can't take secret passageway out of the genius."

Pillover was having none of it. "What does that even mean, you French lunatic?" The years, it seemed, had not materially changed his friend's mischievous character.

They had always been a mismatched pair. Madame Genevieve Lefoux was as mad as engineers could come, with a propensity for ludicrous devices and eccentricity in manner and dress that could not, by rights, be entirely blamed on her nationality. She had, after all, spent the better part of her childhood schooling in England. She had been eager to join in Sophronia's various adventures and larks when she was aboard the finishing school. She had been rather sad when it was just her and Pillover left at Bunson's and much of Sophronia's brand of excitement entirely dissipated. Clearly, Vieve had gone on to university and beyond, with her childish enthusiasm for trouble untempered by the slings and arrows of adult practicalities.

If she was coming to live in London, Pillover was relieved to be well and truly out of the city. Genevieve Lefoux was about to be London's problem, not his.

"You have a child now, I understand?"

"Indeed I do. Quesnel. He's quite too much to cope with and always eager, no matter how sticky the situation."

"Explodes things a lot, does he?"

Vieve made a face.

"Like mother, like—"

"Don't you start, Pill."

"Dimity's got two now, too."

"Does she really? How remarkable. You're the bachelor uncle, are you?"

"That would appear to be the situation."

"Do you think this is big enough to install an ascension chamber? Oh, why am I asking you?" They paused while Vieve did some measuring. Pillover obligingly jotted down the numbers she called at him. Then she resumed their previous conversation. "Are you heading up to hers for the holidays?"

"After this, yes."

"Nottingham or something similar?"

"Nottingham."

Vieve nodded. "And Sophronia?"

"I do not hear of – or from – her."

"Sidheag?"

Pillover shook his head. "And it'd be best not to know Sidheag if you really do intend to stay in London."

"Really, why?"

"You're a member of the OBO, are you not?"

Vieve looked at him. Pillover was pleased to note that he'd actually managed to startle her. He made a note of it in her silly little measurement book, with the date.

"How on earth? Pill, you aren't still playing their game, are you? I thought you were out."

Pillover shook his head, annoyed by the accusation. As if he had ever even pretended to be an intelligencer of any ilk. No, no, he had always been dragged into it by others.

"You have an octopus tattoo on your neck, my friend. Surely you are aware of that fact?"

"Of course I am, you nubbin. But how do you know what it means?"

"Oh, as you say, I'm still a member." He frowned and considered her shocked expression. "It's been absolutely years now. Mostly habit. Agatha put me up to it, no idea why. But regardless, there's something going on with the OBO and the local werewolves. It's not on. You can't be seen to know each other at all. Plus Lord Maccon, London's nearest alpha, is also in contention with Sidheag and her pack."

"Gracious me, why?"

Pillover shrugged. "I've no idea. You should be gratified I know even that much. You know I can't abide London politics, especially not those of the supernatural set. You'll have to ask Sophronia for the details. She'd know. If you can find her."

"Of course she would. Very well, then. And Agatha?"

"I was going to ask you about her. Thought maybe you'd've seen her more recently than I. Being as last I heard, she was visiting France regularly."

Vieve shook her head. "She arranged for me to join the OBO way back when, but I haven't seen her in years. But Pill, you're a classicist. Why would the OBO allow such fraternization?"

"Oh, I translated some Latin medical texts for a while there. Then they forgot to kick me out when I stopped and focused on poetry."

Vieve nodded, still clearly nonplussed. "I thought you hated secret societies."

"Mmm. Like secret passages, hardly worth the bother or the maintenance. And yet, here I stand, a victim of both."

"Still, it's a rummy old thing."

Pillover was resigned to the fact that he would get no current information out of her about Agatha. Vieve seemed to know less than he about their intelligencer friends and their machinations. Perhaps it was about time Vieve returned to England and got all caught up.

"Want to come up with me to Dim's country place?" he asked, knowing his sister wouldn't mind the invitation.

"No, wouldn't be good for her current political standing or sterling reputation, having me visit her. Best if we were not publicly known to be old friends."

Pillover nodded, because Vieve understood these things a grand sight better than he ever would.

"I need to get back to Paris either way. That son of mine, remember? Can't be left for long in the care of a tutor – he's already broken one, burned another, and frightened away the third."

"Active sort of boy, is he?"

"Very."

"You're taking the dirigible back tonight?"

"I am indeed, on the evening breeze."

Pillover nodded. Disappointing. He would be dining at the club alone then.

And so he was.

The Hypocras Club was new enough to boast a fairly experimental French chef, but Pillover ordered the boiled potatoes and mutton chop because he didn't hold with the new cuisine from the Continent, plus he'd had quite enough of the French for one day. There was tarragon in his potatoes and thyme in his peas, which he thought unsporting, but then, many of the members of this club turned out to be younger than himself, so who was he to criticize the tastes of the scientific youth?

He remained suspicious over the nighttime practices of the club, and not just the cuisine. He wondered what his affiliation with the OBO had wrought. Had he not had the discussion with Vieve about secret passageways, he might have taken to his bed with little fuss, as he ought. Instead, he was seized with a quite uncharacteristic curiosity (which happened rarely and was always regretted later) that saw him exploring the bowels of the club after supper on the pretense of looking for the library.

Pillover had always played the bumbling absentminded professor supremely well, even as a very young boy. As he had gotten older, he'd only grown into the role. Like old slippers. His shoulders were now stooped and his spectacles in a permanent state of sliding inexorably down his nose.

The club seemed somewhat proud of its OBO connection, if the frequent use of the octopus motif in decoration was anything to go by. The off-limits part seemed to be nothing more than the obligatory warren of messy studies and lounges required for the smooth running of such an establishment, nothing special. Pillover was about to give up and declare his own instincts in the matter of secrets quite rusty when he happened upon the first of what could only be described as medical laboratories.

There were beds set about, in pairs, with gadgetry and surgeon's tools in between, for what purpose he could only imagine. And Pillover was not that imaginative. The rooms were clean in that way that barbers pretend to cultivate, but there was an undeniable whiff of blood about.

The entire setup gave him a very unpleasant feeling. Even if there was no one in those beds, Pillover suspected he would very much rather not know any more about them.

"You there! What are you doing here?"

Pillover jerked in surprise. "What is this?" he asked, in the affronted tone of an aristocrat who feels himself in the right place at all times by virtue of assumed ownership over everything he surveys.

"Just our medical facilities."

"Why would a club for scientists need such? This is not White's. There are no pugilistic endeavors on the regular, with gentlemen bopping snoots and fencing fists."

"How do you know what entertains the ranks of our members, sir?" The clerk, or whatever he was, was taking Pillover at face value, thank heavens.

Pillover pretended shock at this revelation. "My goodness, are you telling me this place allows the Corinthian set to join? That's not very select, now, is it? I should reconsider my membership under such circumstances. Can't abide a man with muscles. So unsightly."

The clerk gave him a hard stare. "Can I help you find something, *sir*?" He emphasized the *sir* a little too much.

Pillover allowed tetchiness into his tone. "I was looking for the library, of course. Who wouldn't be, after supper? I was directed this way."

"That seems unlikely, sir, since the library is in the opposite direction."

Pillover flapped a hand. "Well, I get muddled with left and right – you know how it is."

"Do I, sir?"

Pillover pretended affront. "Well, take me to it, if you would be so kind. And a snifter of brandy while you're about it." Orders always distracted people.

Accordingly, Pillover felt compelled to sit in the library for a good two hours after that (when he would much rather be reading in bed) drinking brandy (which he had little taste for) just to make a show of it. He was tolerably convinced that he had not gotten away with it, and that he would never be welcomed back to the Hypocras Club. But he also thought, because of their octopus connection to the OBO, that he should tell Agatha something about those strange medical rooms. But what? And how?

It was Dimity who provided the means, rather casually, in fact, a few days later.

"I need to get a message to Agatha, Dim."

"Oh Pill, haven't you given up yet?"

He glared to stop himself from blushing. "It's not that at all. It's something job related."

"Oh?"

"Dimity, you know I can't tell you. Especially if you're out of the game."

"Who says I'm out?"

"Aren't you a respectable patroness now, Lady Dimity Bontwee?"

"*Respectable*, my giddy aunt. Well, if not me, why not Sophronia? You know she still plays."

"And no doubt you see *her* regularly. I'm sorry, no, it was Agatha who started this one, and it's Agatha who needs the information."

Dimity shook her head. "I thought you hated this kind of thing."

"I do."

"You're doing this, why?"

"Because Agatha asked me to a long time ago. And a promise is a promise."

"Pillover, do be careful."

"That is why I'm trying to pass this information on. I shouldn't be the only one holding it."

Dimity sighed. "Oh, very well. I have a letterbox for Ags in London. You can send it to her there." She passed over the address.

Pillover probably should have written the thing in code, but he'd never learned such tricky ways. He just wrote to Agatha to say that he thought the octopuses were on the move and that there were medical experiments of some kind taking place at the Hypocras Club in London, and he would eat his hat if there weren't. Or one of Vieve's hats. Which would likely explode.

Agatha would have to make of that what she would.

Much to his surprise, Agatha wrote back thanking him for the information. She did not explain anything, but what had he expected?

He replied promptly by post to the same address, reminding her of her promise to keep him abreast of her whereabouts, and that her missives had been sporadic and sparse of late.

She wrote back again, a longer letter than he'd received in ages. Saying she always kept her promises and that she was traveling as much as ever, that she missed their talks by the fire, and that she would not think it amiss if he wrote to her, at this post box, with information about a little more of his life, sometimes. The was no plea in her actual words, but the plea was there nevertheless.

And so he did.

Her notes remained short and largely uninformative, but they increased in frequency, which was a relief.

He wrote to her as often as he could, sending into the void where she wasn't, for sometimes it would be months before he got a reply. During the gaps in proper correspondence, he got short notes from foreign lands, which meant she had left before his last letter arrived.

He wrote to her of his monotonous daily life tutoring and translating. He detailed his friends at the linguistics club (Sorrinson's latest passion for breeding cocker spaniels or Fellburt's latest affaire with a widow two times his age who kept bees). Agatha would occasionally ask questions about them, when she found her way home and wrote him back.

It was only nibbles of information and sporadic contact, but it was more than he'd had in years, so Pillover was disposed to treasure it (insignificant though it might seem to an outsider). He took great care with his missives for knowing that they were a kind of balm to her – the kind that had once been fireside chats. He took charge of the duty of reminding her of a safe, mundane world full of cozy realities far removed from her own life.

~

Summer 1877 ~ HMS Nimbus Nugget, in the aetherosphere somewhere over South America

Agatha had many memories of dirigible travel over the years. Since vampires couldn't float, it was often required of their lackeys. She remembered that one time on the *Nimbus Nugget* because she had a private cabin for a change. Ordinarily her cover as an archaeological sketch artist did not warrant such digs. Dirigible travel was rarely luxurious for a spy of her particular talents. But by that summer Lord Akeldama had become the Potentate of the realm, and it had unexpectedly beneficial side effects for even his less well known and carefully forgotten accessories.

She had been tracking a member of the OBO at the time, a retired scientist whose fascination with gourd cultivation and advanced fertilization techniques had apparently led him into the bat guano business. Not in and of itself all that remarkable, except, of course, that his prior field of study had been Chilean saltpeter, and where saltpeter went and guano followed, pyrotechnics inevitably resulted.

Agatha would never have called herself an explosives expert. Not her style at all. Far too loud and flashy. But she recognized the need to know if a new weapons manufacturer was entering an already crowded playing field, and this particular gentleman enjoyed transport by dirigible. In fact, he seemed a little too fascinated with floating for anyone's comfort. His wife had complained in Agatha's sympathetic ear over retsina at a party not two weeks ago. At length. Odds were in favor of his focusing on anti-dirigible munitions, and Agatha did know a lot about dirigibles and the aetherosphere. Mostly because she made regular use of both.

In the security of a private cabin, she remembered wondering if she could write to Pillover. But she was heading *into* trouble, not away from it, and she tried never to write to him until she was leaving something else behind. It was the first time she remembered missing him on a mission, when her attention ought to be on something else. The combination of luxury, safety, and too much leisure made her think of him in a way that was normally reserved for when she was in London. And in thinking of him, she ached for something she had never, and would never, allow herself. First time for that too – realizing she hurt for him, but because of her own choices. That in associating Pillover with her only comfort she had made him into a weakness that she must jealously guard, even from herself. She was guilty of having used him for decades as an anchor to a cozy, friendly world that she had not earned and did not deserve.

CHAPTER ELEVEN
MULLED WINE REUNION

Over the years, Pillover had taken to spending what holidays he could with his sister and her family in Coot's Crest. Their country seat was a smallish Grecian-inspired mansion just outside Nottingham, of the visually extravagant variety built recently with funds earned through dirigible speculation. Sir Crispin had purchased it at a steal when the floating concern went under.

Pillover would never say such a thing to her face, but Dimity kept a fine house with an excellent table and, more to her credit, when it was just the family it vibrated with a comforting if chaotic atmosphere.

It was always loud at her abode. Very loud. Dimity had never lost her propensity for chatter. Her adoring husband indulged her in this overmuch, for he was a relaxed, easygoing fellow, at least where Pillover's sister was concerned. He'd have to be, because Dimity, who had always rather enjoyed doing things to excess, produced no less than five boy children, all of whom were as outgoing and chattery as she. Hence the loudness.

Pillover abhorred them all, of course. Which meant he

visited frequently and was naturally to be found most evenings in the nursery, covered in wooden cars and snotty boy children and all manner of disturbingly fond things. They were horrible little blighters – always dashing about, yelling, and throwing themselves with utter abandon at their Uncle Pill demanding dirigible carries and rough play. Pillover, who was a weak man, after a token protest always accommodated them with alacrity. And maybe a tiny part of it was the love in those thin sun-browned arms wrapping tight about his neck and the noisy joy of home, but he would never admit that to anyone, least of all his sister.

He always brought his nephews *books* as presents, of course. He wasn't *that* weak.

∼

December 1880 ~ A very loud nursery at Coot's Crest, Nottingham

Agatha was in Nottingham to check on a werewolf pack, and it was pure whim that caused her to remember that Dimity's country residence was nearby. She was at loose ends and it was Christmas or she really wouldn't have bothered.

Had she known Pillover was visiting, too, she definitely wouldn't have bothered – for his protection or for hers, she wasn't sure which. His letters had become a kind of tether over the years. The first thing she did upon returning to London was to go to the little postal receiving box she paid dearly to be kept by someone very discreet in a dead person's name. The letters waiting for her there were just so very *him*. Full of complaints about petty academic matters, and Latin phrases she'd have to look up to understand, and occasionally some snippet of a poem he'd recently translated. They were full of superficial gossip about his colleagues who, she suspected, were actually friends, and whose personalities she could easily guess at because she knew Pillover so well and she could imagine all the details missing from his descriptions.

She didn't need to see him face to face again after so long, knowing all the intimacy of his life that he had shown her with his pen. That would be too much – too unequal a relationship, when she persisted in sharing so little. It was as if what had once been a one-sided love affair had become a one-sided friendship.

And then she called upon his sister.

She should have known better than to do anything spontaneously. She was not a spontaneous person and thus was unequivocally bad at it. In addition, she should have realized that it was Christmas and they were family.

Dimity's house was altogether too noisy and full of holiday cheer. All the things one expected of the season were in evidence – fresh pine boughs tied to banisters, and an overabundance of candlelight, dangling silver bells, and the scent of mulled wine.

Agatha came in through the servants' entrance, because she always did. She hated to announce herself. Even though she'd never been to the house before, she knew the style and she knew the kind of person Dimity was, and the type of visitors she still received who would also choose a back entrance.

She slipped though the scullery and into the delivery passage, neatly avoiding the busy staff, and up the stairs to the family apartments, which seemed the source of most of the noise.

There was an open door to a large nursery. Dimity stood in the square of light, next to her husband, her golden head on his shoulder and his arm about her waist. It was as if they were posing for some French painter. They were in casual dress, comfortably loose and unrefined, and Dimity's hair was down. They clearly did not anticipate company that evening and were expecting an early night.

Agatha moved to stand next to and a little behind Dimity, peeking in over her friend's shoulder.

Absolute chaos reigned in that nursery, which Agatha supposed was only to be expected with five children. Really, what had her friend been thinking? *Five* of them, all boys. So excessive.

There were toys everywhere, and boys everywhere, and there seemed more than five in that room, but that was the nature of boys in motion. There was a tutor of some species playing with them.

Agatha debated how to make herself known.

But Dimity, clearly, had not relaxed all her training even as she left the field of play, for she saw Agatha out of the corner of her eye. Agatha was not wearing a dress that matched to the wallpaper and she hadn't been trying to hide either way.

"Well, this is an unexpected pleasure. Good evening, my dear," said her old school chum.

The new husband – although Agatha supposed it had been a decade now – looked over in response to his wife's softly spoken greeting.

Agatha and Sir Crispin had met many times and she still did not entirely understand him. Which made her suspect him, of course. But he adored her friend with a kind of fervent, permissive love that was rare in men of his ilk, and Agatha was disposed to like him for that. Even love him a little.

He had apparently grown very comfortable over the years with lady spies showing up in his house unannounced. Agatha assumed that he must be equally sanguine about the sudden appearance of an Alpha werewolf and her pack or a mad inventor and her boon female companion. Agatha could not help but admire a man who put up with extremes of eccentricity – the residual effect of their kind of education. Under such circumstances five boy children, she suspected, were a mere trifle.

"Ah," said Sir Crispin, "Miss Woosmoss, how nice. You're just in time for mulled wine. Just let us get these pikelets to bed. Wife, where's the nursemaid?"

"Goodness, how on earth should I know? Just let Pillover do it. You know he prefers it anyway when he's here."

Agatha took a second look at the tutor, who was currently under a pile of what looked to be three of Dimity's holy terrors.

Floppy dark hair in need of a cut, a handsome sullen face, skin too pale from a life spent indoors, spectacles of a sturdy nature. He looked much as he always had – only older.

The face that looked up at her fractured into something part wonder, part pain for just a moment, before it resumed its normal longsuffering, morbid expression.

"All right, you monsters, off!" he said, surfacing out of the tangled limbs of children. They screamed in hilarity and transferred their clinging to his legs so that he had to wade towards the door through them as if through a peat bog. They seemed not to know or care that his attention was fixed on something else.

Sir Crispin, because he was a perceptive man, said, "Pillover, old chap, why not show our guest to the mulled wine while the wife and I see to our progeny."

"Must we?" said the wife in question. "This is way more interesting."

"Now, now, Sparkles, be generous."

"You're no fun sometimes, you know that, my darling heart?"

Sir Crispin hustled his wife into the nursery. Dimity went to corral some of the children, while he concentrated on transferring the others from Pillover's legs to his own.

Eventually Pillover was free and without a word of greeting, he tilted his head at Agatha and led her back downstairs to the family parlor where, in grand holiday fashion, there was indeed a small cauldron of mulled wine sitting over a cheery fire.

Pillover ladled out a mug for her with shaking hands and without asking if she wanted any. He filled one for himself, nodding for her to sit. He clutched his drink in both hands and stared into the liquid, sneaking little furtive glances at her as if he were thirsty for her face and not the wine.

Agatha felt her shoulders lower for the first time in a decade. She put the wine to one side without drinking any. Then, boneless, she folded down to sit on the rug in front of the fire, scooted back and around until she was leaning against his legs, and pulled her own into her chest.

After a long moment, his fingers were in her hair, tentative, loosening it from the tight knot that was customary for her more covert operations. He worked the pins free and the locks loose, combing through and massaging her scalp the way he had once loved to do, as if no time had passed at all. As if it were late at night and they were back in an obscure London townhouse.

Agatha found herself crying for absolutely no reason. Just soft, steady tears, not sorrow, more relief. A valve that had been opened again after too long was allowing the dirigible to rise, allowing air back into her lungs.

He leaned forward in his chair, draped himself down, long wiry arms coming around her shoulders, crossing over her collarbone. She put her hands up to catch his, still so soft and bony. He kissed her wet cheek, then rested his chin on the top of her head.

She had missed him so much, with every part of her body. Her skin prickled at the familiar smell of him, and her heart sounded like some old dirty carpet being beaten under the sun. He had been there all along and she had ached for him and never acknowledged the hole that ache created in her, because the knowing of it would have made everything that much worse. Now she couldn't avoid the simple truth that she had missed him and missed this.

The thudding in her chest was returning her home, the rhythmic pull of an anchor winching down to catch and hold. She had untied them both to unmoor herself. But he was like some rock that had waited, calm and steady, for her to tether to it again. And if she untied herself tomorrow, he would still wait. How stupid of her never to have realized that. He, who had not changed in his steadfastness of purpose or interest or intent all his life, would certainly not change in his devotion to her, even for his own good. That this careful life she had constructed for him, that she had needed him to have without her, with someone else, was all a fantasy of her making to comfort herself. Because without her, he was only ever going to wait.

She tilted her head back to catch his lips upside down, from salty cheek to sweet mouth, and gave him everything she could think of to hold on to, so he might cling to her transience.

She would grasp onto just this, if it was all they got to have. If it was all she was allowed. His hands cupping her chin. Him tasting like mulled wine and her tasting like regret.

∼

"You don't want to come back with me, do you, Agate? To Oxford?" Pillover worked up the courage to ask her, later, in his arms in a tangle of sheets and hope.

"No, I don't think so."

Pillover tugged at his ear. "It's not like it once was. I'm not in dingy chambers in halls anymore. I've got a proper little cottage. It's not in the best part of town, but it is right between the rail station and the landing green. I thought at least there you would like it better. Ease of escape and all that."

"Very thoughtful, Pill, but I don't think you should have taken me into account on such a personal matter."

"I always take you into account."

She gave a tiny smile. "Mmm. You're the only one who does. It's why I can't ever shake you."

"So will you come see it?"

"No."

Pillover nodded. He hadn't really expected otherwise. "Maybe sometime you'll have an assignment down there."

"Even if I did, I wouldn't involve you or our home."

"*Our* home?"

"Even if I never see it, I'll think of it that way."

"You're a very strange woman, Agate."

"I know."

He tilted his head, understanding. "Are you afraid that if you come, you won't want to leave?"

"Mmm."

"That would be bad?"

"There's still so much left to do. So many places I haven't seen."

"Come anyway."

She didn't, but Pillover felt better for having extended the invitation. And he hoped against hope that she understood what he really meant by it. That he would continue to wait and that it was perfectly fine for her to take as long as she needed to remember he was there by the fire, safe and warm.

∾

Winter 1885 ~ Oxford, a small cottage halfway between the rail station and the dirigible green

It took Agatha five years to work up the courage to go see him. Or maybe it wasn't courage, exactly, more simple yearning.

One cold winter day, she came back from almost six months abroad to her dilapidated little bedsit in a newly constructed complex occupied mainly by clerks and day workers. London, the queen of industry, was laboring under a fog like pea soup, and the smell of black dust and coal was all around her.

Agatha hated it.

This last trip, she'd seen waterfalls so tall they created four rainbows on the way down, and behind them she'd been tied up and beaten for the information stored only in her brain. Her nose had been broken in the process and, without question, what few looks she'd ever had, were long since gone. Silly to be upset mostly about that last bit. Agatha had never had much appearance to lose and she was old enough that such things should no longer concern her. She could no longer trade on anything but her skill and experience. Which is what she should take pride in. But still she stood in front of the clouded old mirror and touched the bump in her nose. These days, parts of her hurt not because of new injuries, but because of old ones.

And she hated London.

She hated where she had to stay in London, alongside all the other forgotten people. She resented Lord Akeldama for forcing her to return at all. That even bruised and beaten and tied up, she would rather be four rainbows deep in a foreign land than where she was now.

So she told her vampire firmly after her report that she was not staying in London ever again. That she was not ready for a new assignment, because she really did need a place to rest for a while. That she was going to stay with an old friend.

Lord Akeldama was surprised without showing it – only Agatha heard it in his voice. He called her a *precious wilted flower* and told her with pained sympathy that *of course* she should rest. As if he somehow remembered when he himself needed such a frivolous thing as a break from London.

Agatha dragged herself to the train station and contemplated whether she should go all the way to Scotland to Sidheag and her pack, or just up to Nottingham to Dimity and her family. But instead of either of those things, Agatha Woosmoss, the Wallflower, boarded a train to Oxford. Due to their many letters over the years, she knew the address by heart, and she found herself at the end of a very long day, on the stoop of a pretty little cottage within walking distance of the station, with a smoking chimney. Soft golden light streamed from the windows, and the sounds of a merry gathering crept out from under the door. Piano music tinkled lightly and occasionally there was the sound of laughter.

Maybe what Pillover *hadn't* written to her about his little cottage was the wife who had come with it. And maybe this was a dinner party and at the table would be a young boy with dark hair and a moody expression, with his father's sad, kind eyes, and Agatha would be breaking something beautiful and solid with her desperate need for a landing place.

Why *had* she come here?

But she was so very tired and the only thing she could think of was sitting with him in front of a fire. Curling up on a rug and leaning back against his legs. Putting her head back onto his knees like she'd once done so many times it became ordinary and not precious. Of his fingers threading through her hair. The way he'd pick up her hand and carefully kiss the crescent at the base of her thumbnail.

Certainly it was petty and weak and selfish to show up on his doorstep after a decade of a few measly letters and one night of mulled wine five years ago just because she hated London and she loved him. But Agatha still pulled the bell and waited for someone to come and break her heart.

It was Pillover who answered. His eyes were bright, and cheeks rosy with wine and song and company. His friends were over, she realized. Those friends he adored and complained about at length who assembled every Wednesday night to talk of more things, these days, than just linguistics. Here in this cozy, cheerful, welcoming house, he'd lost some of his patented moroseness.

The moment he realized who it was, his face lost all its color. Agatha was devastated that just seeing her had done that to him.

Even as she turned to melt away into the shadows, he grabbed her wrist and tugged her inside. "Agate."

Just like that, the years were gone again, and his soft hand was on her face, and his eyes were making mathematical calculations of her bruises. She knew he saw the stiffness in her walk. Being tied up in a cave under a waterfall will do that to a girl.

His thumb slid under her cuff to feel the raised edges of the rope burns there.

"You have company," she said, softly, so no one might overhear. "I should go."

"No!" He almost shouted it. "I'll make them go instead."

"Not on my account, please. I could wait somewhere else for a while."

"Where would you go in Oxford at this time of night, looking like that? Where should you go but here? Stay."

"But—" She gestured – laughter from the sitting room, the piano striking up a polka.

"None of that matters. Not now that you're here right in front of me. Please don't go away again. I can hardly believe it." It was such an un-Pilloverian thing to say, and so desperate it paused her panic with concern for his.

She shifted her weight as if preparing for a fight, unsure of what to do – in his house, in his territory, where she had never been before. "What should I—?"

"Go upstairs. There's a spare room to the right at the end of the hall. Put your stuff there. Oh, of course, it's you, no stuff. It shouldn't take long to get rid of them. It's only old friends."

"Spare room? Not your— There is, maybe, a wife? Family?" Spare room. Of course he would want her in a spare room.

"What wife? No wife. Don't go, Agate. Hang the spare room, go to *my* room. I don't care – whatever gets you to stay."

"You shouldn't have to accommodate my idiosyncrasies."

"Please. Just this once, do as I ask. Please." He sounded so desperate that it shook her out of her inability to cope with the situation that she had wrought. How had she never learned to avoid spontaneity?

She nodded. "Very well."

"Promise you'll stay long enough for me to see you. Don't just go upstairs and then change your mind and disappear."

She looked at him hard.

"Promise me, Agate."

She ground her teeth. "I promise."

He breathed out in relief. "Excellent. Good. Very well. I'll just go, make them leave as quickly as possible."

How very like Pillover to extract a promise from her. He knew what those were worth.

Upstairs, in his room, because of course she went there – spare bedroom indeed! – she found something that she could not bear to understand. A row of agates on the windowsill like sentries, waiting patiently for her.

∼

It was different this time. Agatha had come to him and it seemed to open some willingness inside her, for after that she started coming regularly. Or as regularly as was natural to her and her profession.

Agatha always went first to London, he assumed, and made her reports, and then caught a train and came to him.

That counted for a whole lot.

Pillover would no more take away Agatha's purpose than she would his dusty books and Latin translations. In this, at least, they understood each other. He did wonder, sometimes, if she asked him to give it all up, if he would. If he could abandon all this work, all his passion for obscure texts and dead languages. Just walk away from his hard fought and maintained position as scholar and academic and teacher. What was his reputation and his position really worth to him? Would he leave it to dwell in the shadows with her, where secrets were kept and there was no glory in publication, only ruination?

He had thought so once. He'd asked her once, when he was young enough to think of letting go of ambition as romantic. She had said no then. He thought that if the tables were turned and she asked him to go, he would probably say no now. Not out of revenge, but out of common sense. But she would never ask such a thing of him, so he likely would never know how far his own common sense stretched when tempered by desire for the impossible.

There were days, though, when he stared at the small desk in the corner with the very thick lock, which he'd purchased because she liked her privacy. Or the thick rug in front of his fireplace that was free of her little chubby feet and the way she liked to scrunch up her toes, barefoot even in winter. He thought sometimes the ache of absence was worse than any loss of identity or purpose that following her entailed. But he knew from experience he was a terrible intelligencer. What more could he be for her than what he already was? Some dream of companionship that she kept locked away, just one of many treasured secrets that she might pull out and reexamine in dark times to remind her that she was human, and that somewhere out in the world, far away, there was one person who loved her.

So he didn't ask her to stay any more or any longer than she could. And he never asked her to marry him again. He learned to appreciate the nuggets of time that she allowed him. Like sunflower seeds eaten one at a time, careful of the hard shell, rare and precious.

He managed a great achievement. He convinced her to sit for a photograph – just one, and just her. He wrote no name or date on the image, and he promised he would show it to no one. He kept it tucked under the largest of the agates, did not frame it or put it on display, not even in his private bedroom. But it was a thing he could take out and look at to remind him that she existed, so that he might have her presence more often than she allowed. A compromise of a kind.

He reconciled himself to the fact that seeing her once in a while and at unpredictable times was better than never seeing her at all. For he had been through that, too, and it was a famine that carved grooves into his heart. If gifted the choice, he would never be without her again. A little bit was better than nothing. And what he received in return was far more than what anyone else ever got, because the point of his Agate was that no one ever saw her at all.

CHAPTER TWELVE
A VERY MATURE AFFAIRE

And so it went for ten years. Good years. Steady years for Professor Pillover Plumleigh-Teignmott. Years full of successes and failures, endless publications and a not insignificant reputation in a very small field, some rewarding students and some terrible ones, and good friends with questionable marriages and then deaths. All of it broken into by Agatha, showing up late at night, letting herself in with no need for a key. Staying for some amount of time never long enough and then leaving again. A pebble dropped into the still lake that was his life.

Pillover thought, reading her latest note, which had been sent from India, which meant she was now even further east, that he was her reward to herself. It was as though she *allowed* herself him, as if he were some gift for a job well done. A special treat she got to have for being a good intelligencer. At least he was special to her, even if he was so special as to be savored in small doses, like some rare and expensive candy. Who but his Agate would dare limit the human heart?

He had grown to cherish certain things over the years.

The little sigh she always made when she arrived and settled against him for the first time. Just a puff of air, like shock and relief. The very quiet, very small version of a steamer train coming to rest at his doorstep. Sometimes she would give this sigh as she climbed into his bed. Sometimes he would just look up for a book to find her there, settled in front of his fire just like the old days. Once she came and curled on the floor next to his desk, tilting sideways against his leg. He had a rug there now, just in case. And always that small sigh. Like tea in from the cold.

One time he looked up from his morning paper and there she was. It was unusual for her to arrive at a respectable hour. Generally speaking, she was a night creature. He stared at her in delight over the top of the paper.

"Ah, good, you again." He tried not to smile too widely.

"You're never surprised to see me, are you, Pill?"

"Never."

She gave her small sigh and propped her chin in one hand. Stole a bit of bacon off his plate.

She looked tired.

"Did you get it done?" He pushed the plate towards her.

"What done?"

"Whatever it was that needed to be done this time?"

"Of course I did. All of it."

"Best girl."

"Mmm."

Later that night, when they were curled up in bed together, he kissed the scar on her left breast that he hated. Partly because he had a proprietary interest in her breasts, but mostly because it had come so close to killing her. He knew that she hated it, too, for different reasons.

She'd come home that time with it pinked and newly healed and when he'd asked her about it, she'd said what she always said. "I miscalculated."

For Agatha, scars were a permanent record of errors in mathematics, geometric failures. Her body had become a ledger for the mistakes of her profession. He kissed every single scar every time he could, counted them up, recorded them out of fear that next time he would find another one.

She put a hand to his chin, scruffy with the beard he couldn't be bothered to shave anymore. "That tickles."

He pressed his chin (and his prickles) into her sternum, brushed it back and forth to see if he could get a pink mark there. Easy to do – she was a redhead, after all, and pinked up easily. He reminded himself that meant she would scar easily, too.

She laughed at him and pressed two fingers to his forehead to get him to rotate, fall against her, and look up at her. "Why is that, Pill?"

"Why is what, Agate?"

"Why is it that you are never surprised when I arrive? When I do that thing where I just appear out of the wallpaper. Everyone else is always surprised to see me."

"When you let them see you, you mean."

"So?" she prodded, brushing at the cheek whiskers at the top of his beard, clearly fascinated by the place where the hair was and was not.

"Because I always expect you to be there."

"But most of the time, I'm not."

"I know. It's the absence that I find surprising." What he didn't add was that this was also when he missed her most. Every time he looked up from his paper, or book, or awoke in an empty bed. He missed her. Dozens of times a day he thought to tell her something, and dozens of times at night he reached for the warm body that wasn't there.

She had white in her eyebrows now. The red had never been very dark there, and now they'd faded so much she looked a touch surprised most of the time. He thought they were dear silken points of memory – time made physical. When he did not see them, or her, it was as though he might be the one forgotten, in his confined little life full of inconsequential things for which she had very little time but immeasurable patience.

When she was home and curled against him, she laughed into his shoulder about the ridiculousness of this don or that one. She loved his endless complaints about the mundanities of teaching, and the petty machinations of chancellors and academic politics. He was shocked she put up with it, tolerated him, as an old friend and lover.

He always expected, the next time she let herself in, that it would be the last. Because the other thing about age was, neither of them were as good at their jobs as they had once been. For a classicist, that meant he sometimes forgot his references and his students laughed at him. But for a spy?

∼

Christmas 1895 ~ Coot's Crest, Nottingham

She'd never been gone so long before. It had been nearly a year with no letters at all. Pillover was so worried he decided to do the unthinkable – involve his sister.

"Dim, can I talk to you?" It was late, the boys long since abed. Sir Crispin was looking sleepy. The big man was sprawled back on a settee not entirely comfortable with its current burden. His brother-in-law was taking up most of the delicate piece of furniture, but in that controlled way of his that spoke of physical fitness, even as the settee objected to the general distribution of the weight. It was odd to see Sir Crispin not moving. He always seemed to be up and about. Dimity was perched next to her husband embroidering something covert and possibly deadly. She looked up, magnification spectacles perched at the end of her nose, making round, distorted smudges out of her cheeks.

"And what exactly have you been doing with me for the past hour if not talking? Singing a dirge?"

Sir Crispin understood. He stretched languidly and rose with easy grace. "I'm for bed." He kissed his wife on the forehead. "Don't be too late?"

"What? Oh? Oh." Dimity wrinkled her pert nose to try to get her specs up without having to put down her needle. "Good night, dear."

Pillover stared at his hands. Silence stretched between them for a long moment. He looked up to find his sister glaring at him.

"Well?" she pressed.

"I haven't had a letter from her in a year."

"Letter? From whom?"

"The Wallflower."

"You correspond regularly, do you?"

Pillover's scalp tickled, but he pushed on anyway. "Yes, we do. Or we have done. Usually it's just a note from whatever foreign clime she's recently left. Which means wherever she is now, she's been stuck there a long while. I'm really worried, Dim."

Dimity nodded, and put aside her embroidery. "Atypical behavior is always concerning. I didn't realize you kept such a close record of her comings and goings." She shook her head at his (no doubt) pained expression and became all businesslike. "The last communication you received, where was it from?"

"India."

"And do you know which direction she was headed, from the general tenor of previous missives?"

"Further east."

Dimity nodded. "You'll get me all the ones prior? They might be useful."

Pillover produced the letters in question with their various foreign stamps and range of paper sizes and styles. Every aspect of these told a story of origin, including the ink. He handed them to his sister, feeling frightened that they might be the last record he had of his Agate. Still, he knew Dimity and her contacts would need everything he could possibly provide to track someone of Agatha's caliber.

"And have you talked to her patron?"

Pillover shook his head. It wasn't that he disliked Lord Akeldama, it was just that he didn't feel he had any right to go asking after a vampire's business based solely on the strength of a one-sided affection for that man's most effective tool. Because that was how Lord Akeldama thought of Agatha. Because that was how vampires were – humans were either useful or they were food, and that was it. Asking Lord Akeldama where Agatha had been sent and what she had been tracking was like barging into the man's home and asking him about his plumbing and why he needed a drain unclogged. Not done. Certainly not by Pillover.

Dimity puffed out her cheeks. "There's an upcoming assembly of note we can capitalize upon, and younger assets in need of targeting, I'll pull in the Wicker Chicken and see what we can do."

Something loosened in Pillover's chest. If Dimity was putting Sophronia on the job, something was bound to be unearthed. Or someone. She would find Agatha or Agatha's body, and either way he would know. Pillover might dislike Sophronia's methods and he might loathe her penchant for adventure, but no one could deny the effectiveness of a strategically applied Wicker Chicken.

Pillover pushed his own spectacles up his nose to

disguise the glistening there. Relief was a rummy old emotion – so often it came out as tears rather than smiles.

"You won't go yourself?"

Dimity shook her head. "We're taking delivery of something here. I must stay to receive it personally."

She was being mysterious. Pillover knew better than to pry.

"The problem is," his sister added, making him tense again, "the person we're most likely to deploy to find her doesn't know what she looks like."

Pillover had anticipated that, too. He understood that Sophronia would be unwilling to go far afield on a wild Agatha chase. She had her own operations and concerns already in motion locally. Sidheag couldn't leave Britain either, something to do with her pack and military service. Dimity wouldn't anymore, because of her family, and Vieve hadn't the skill set. He'd figured they would need to send someone else. And that someone would need to know what they were looking for.

He reached into his breast pocket and pulled out his one photograph of Agatha. She looked serious and stern and a little matronly. He loved that photograph. He'd promised her that he would never show it to anyone. He'd said he'd never allow it to be connected with any of her names. He was betraying her for the first and, he hoped, only time.

He handed it over.

Dimity stared at it, taking in the worn edges from his handling it over the years. Her mouth twisted. "How long, Pill?"

Pillover wondered if that was sympathy on her face. Which hurt. But he knew exactly what she was asking. "How old am I now?"

"Let me see. I'm fifty-seven, almost fifty-eight, so you must be fifty-five or so."

"So then, forty years, I guess, give or take a few."

"What?"

"We never made it official, but I've been faithful and I think maybe she has, too. You know how she is. Quiet."

"Reticent."

"Loyal," Pillover corrected. Agatha's loyalty was partly to her own desires, her own wanderlust needs, but that was a kind of loyalty.

"Yes, that, too. Oh but Pill, how awful, in secret all this time." Which was an odd thing for his sister to say, who had spent most of her life dabbling in secrets and the shadow worlds that housed them. As if a secret love were any more or less significant than the regular full-sunshine kind of steady affection.

"I always knew what I was getting into, remember? I grew up with your lot. Secrecy is your profession, after all." He smiled. "I did ask her to marry me, once."

"Did you really? What did she say?" As if that answer weren't perfectly obvious.

Pillover rolled his eyes at her, just like the old days when they were children. "She said no. Evidently."

"Did she? No secret marriage, then?"

Pillover shouldn't have dignified that with a response, and yet… "Maybe a little bit. I figured that was it, you see? I meant it wholeheartedly when I asked. So I just stayed married to her – in my head, anyway. She comes home when she can. And when she does, she comes to me. In Oxford. Which she never did before. It's enough."

"Is it?" Dimity frowned. "I always wondered, you know? Why you never married. I mean, you've always been a grumpy old thing, but I thought maybe someone once broke your heart and so you just *pined*."

"Pretty much."

"Poor old Pill. You love her, then?"

"Hard to remember a time when I did not."

"Did you tell her that part?"

"Why? Do you think it's important?"

"Oh, really, Pill!"

"It wouldn't make a difference, Dim."

"How do you know?"

"I just do. And I don't want to make it any harder for her to return."

"To leave you behind, you mean?"

"No, to come back to me. Better these things are left unsaid, so that I can be the place she feels safest. The place she rests."

"You're a limp noodle, is what you are."

Pillover shrugged. "At least I'm tasty and sustaining."

~

Spring 1896 ~ The Spotted Custard dirigible, headed home from Japan

The journey back to London on the *Spotted Custard* was delightfully uneventful. Agatha had her own cabin, which was luxurious and restful and granted her far too much time to dwell on the past and Pillover's part in it. If her life were a measuring tape, his presence could be measured out in prime numbers. They floated into London's dirigible landing green in Hyde Park on a rainy spring evening with more fanfare than usual, because this ship was captained by Prudence Akeldama Maccon Tarabotti Lefoux after all. Or whatever her name was now. There were many people invested in her safety and the safety of her crew. Lord Akeldama had sent drones and an ornate carriage to meet her. Baroness Tunstell had also sent drones and an even more ornate carriage. Agatha recognized at least two faces in the small crowd waiting for the dirigible, faces whom she only knew by code name.

There was no one waiting for Agatha, of course. Or there was, but he was back in Oxford and it would take her some while to get to him. She waited while a fuss was made and everyone disembarked, or didn't, according to their natures and loyalty to the ship.

Finally, after the crowd had dispersed but before the gangplank was raised, she trotted easily down it, small pack over one shoulder, nothing else needed. She wished for her oiled greatcoat. She always forgot how rainy London was.

She left the green for the walkway towards the hack stands, the dripping darkness oddly friendly for once.

A voice out of the shadows startled her.

"Terribly careless of me, to meet the love of my life at twelve and then spend the rest of my days misplacing her."

"Pillover?" She turned and stared.

"Ah, did I surprise you? How wonderful. The one and only time, I suspect." He approached, but not too close, hands stuffed down into his pockets, shoulders slumped.

"You came to London to meet me?"

"I know, not part of our arrangement, but you were gone a *very* long time, Agate."

His face was shrouded by a soggy-looking top hat and he was shivering, for he too had no coat. Agatha wondered how long he'd been waiting in the rain, and worried, because he was a fragile old thing. He hadn't her training in matters of survival.

"Over a *year*." He sounded petulant.

"But you know I always come back to you, Pill. Eventually."

"Agate." His voice was very serious. "I thought you were dead."

Agatha realized what he was really saying. "You sent them after me. Or you activated the Wicker Chicken on my behalf."

"Please don't be angry."

Agatha considered. She wasn't angry. In fact, she was oddly flattered. She'd gone missing and everyone she loved had set out to find her again. Even Pillover, who could do nothing but sit back and beg others for aid. But he had done that for her, because he worried. Because he loved her.

She was old and tired and had just spent too long on an airship surrounded by children who had a better grasp of love and family than she ever would. Yet here was this boy, now a man, now grey at the temples, who understood but had never pushed until now.

He bowed his head. "I gave them your photograph."

Agatha nodded. "I guessed as much. They knew what I looked like. Arsenic and Percy, when they first encountered me. No one knows what I look like. Ever. It was a first."

"I broke my promise."

"You did. And what punishment should I mete out for that?"

"You wrote me no letters for a *year*."

"Are you perhaps implying that I broke my promise, too?"

"Yes, for the first time."

"So we give each other a pass, just this once?"

"Do we?" Even in the dark and the rain she could see the hope in him.

Agatha wondered if he had come to meet her here and confess his sin right away so that she would not waste time traveling to Oxford only to hate him for this one infraction. "I'm firm in my resolve, Pill, but I'm not a harsh person."

"I know. It is one of the things I love about you."

Agatha had not missed that he was using that word. That something had broken in him during this past year and he no longer cared to be delicate with their relationship. He thought he had lost her and now, he would cling all the tighter. Perhaps she was finally ready to accept that. Because if the *Spotted Custard*'s insane crew had taught her anything, it was that love was no limit on freedom. Affection was not a disguise for obligation. Love just *was*, and sometimes it drifted about the world on a dirigible and sometimes it waited patiently in the rain.

∼

Spring 1896 ~ Oxford

Agatha could count her time on this earth in the silver threads at Pillover's temples. She knew, without embarrassment, that he could do the same with her, only there was more time to count as she had seen more of this earth and had more grey hair.

"You were right, you know, back then," Pillover said, as if picking up a conversation he'd had with himself. He did that kind of thing now – absentminded professor in more than just appearance. He had become what he always pretended to be. What he always wanted to be. They both had.

"Back when?" she encouraged him, head on his knee, curled before a fire, the rain beating its restful symphony into Oxford outside.

"When we were young and I accused you of practicing your wiles on me. Toying with my emotions." He stopped petting her hair and rested his hand on her shoulder. "I was such a dramatic child. Do you remember what you said?"

"I do not."

"You said that I would never know the truth of your heart because you would never be around long enough for me to find it out. I thought you were cruel at the time. I realized, later, that you were warning me off. You were telling me then the reality of loving you. That there was room for me, but not very much."

She raised her hand to cover his.

"But now I think it was also a promise to yourself. A vow you sent into the world, that no one should break the sanctity of your restlessness."

"You've been reading too much Latin poetry again. Or is it that new philosopher friend of yours – what's his name?"

He ignored this. "You told me, that day, what was really in your heart and I was too blind to see it."

Agatha didn't want him to be hard on himself for her past actions. "Not blind. What person truly knows, at seventeen, what she wants out of life?"

"Well, you. You did." He turned his hand over, grasped hers, still resting on her shoulder.

"True."

"And I. I knew then that I wanted you, and I was even younger." He rubbed at her calluses with his thumb. Calluses from the crossbow of her youth, the knives of her middling years, and the newest ones from those oars in that appalling little boat that she'd rowed for days and days. Where had that been? She couldn't remember now.

"Nobody falls in love forever when they're barely out of the schoolroom, Pillover. That's either profound laziness or an utter lack of imagination."

"And yet, here I am, forty-odd years later." He raised her hand to his lips and kissed the crescent moon at the base of her thumbnail. A classic Pillover thing to do. What had he once called it? Ah yes, a leftover deposit of ancient divinity. How had she remembered that, a decades-gone throwaway comment, and forgotten a whole sea in which she'd been stranded just this past year?

"You're just stubborn," she accused.

"And you aren't?"

"What a pair we make."

"I've always thought so."

"Have we both been too stubborn, Pill?" She was really worried. Had her drive to move and be lost destroyed something for both of them, something better than what little they'd had?

"Perhaps. I learned to wait for the moments when you drifted my way and cherish them." He let go her hand and resumed swirling her hair between his fingertips.

"And I learned how to pause on occasion." Perhaps that was good. Perhaps in only seeing him sometimes, that was how they'd lasted so long. Like a slow-acting poison.

"I think we've done pretty well, all told." He mirrored her thoughts.

"Do you, really?"

"Both of us got a lifetime of love. What does it matter that it was eked out in small doses? That it does not look at all as the storybooks said it ought?"

She swiveled, leaned an elbow on his knee, and looked up at him. "Thank you for always waiting."

"And thank you for always coming back... eventually."

"I was thinking of staying around for a while."

He took a shaky breath. "How long this time?"

She tucked her courage beneath her breastbone and pulled out her heart. "Maybe, perhaps, forever?"

He folded down onto her, kissed her temple, and didn't say anything.

She thought she had made the worst blunder yet, that

this was a silence she was now owed for having dared to push at their established pattern. She let the quiet stretch, patient with it, and carefully put her heart back where it deserved to be, unoffered.

"Too much?" she asked, finally.

"No." His voice was round and coarse and damp and shaken. "It's just — I'd almost given up."

"I don't understand."

"Agatha Woosmoss, I have loved you since I was in knee britches."

"But…"

"No, it really is that simple."

"Oh." And here she'd spent a lifetime running around thinking she was unloved and unlovable. Not pretty enough. Not smart enough. Not vibrant enough. Not enough. Yet she hadn't diminished herself. Not really. It was worse. She'd diminished him. Because if he had loved her for all these years – really loved her – and she hadn't seen it, hadn't noticed, she'd been silently telling him all along that she wasn't worthy and that he was stupid for feeling anything.

He pressed a wet face into her neck.

She rubbed her cheek into his dark hair. The grey was coarser, rougher against her skin, full of memories. "I hurt you."

"For a very long time."

"I'll stop now."

"Oh? How is that?"

"I'll stay."

"You promise."

"I promise."

"And you always keep your promises."

EPILOGUE

Pillover remained, decidedly absentmindedly as the years went on, a founding member of the OBO. They trotted him out for ceremonies requiring the accurate recitation of Latin verse and invited him to only the most necessary events. And because it had become habit, and Pillover was ever a creature of habit, he attended.

He was old.

They were old.

They had mostly stopped caring about everything, as you do when you're quite old. Agatha's hair was white and she wore it short out of annoyance. Pillover's was not only white but nearly absent. Her calluses had become liver spots and his memories were all dust motes. Their cozy cottage was cluttered with things they kept because they couldn't remember not to.

Agatha stayed involved with vampires and information and the business of empires, of course she did. But mostly with her pen. With her affinity for modern languages and his for dead ones, there were always things to translate and codes to break requiring discretion. And Agatha was nothing if not discreet.

For his part, Pillover paid more attention to the activities of the brass octopus than he let on, because he had promised his Agate that he would. He, too, was a man who kept his promises. So when he unearthed their plans to build hundreds of explosive mines and seed the aetherosphere with them, it was Agatha he told about it.

When Agatha came up with the counter plan to ensure most of those mines failed and did not in fact explode, it was the two of them, at some seventy years of age or more, breaking into a massive warehouse on the eve of war.

Maybe they only managed to sabotage half of them. But later, after many years had passed, the scientists who study such things determined that enough of them had failed for the aether to survive, in a different form. The world had burned and changed, but it had not been wholly destroyed. And it most certainly *should* have been.

Perhaps everyone forgot, if they ever knew, that there was a secret society involved, but these things are easy to overlook. They're called *secret* for a reason.

And perhaps this is all a different story.

Promises. Promises.

fin

AUTHOR'S NOTE

Thank you so much for reading my little offering. If you enjoyed it, or if you would like to read more about any of my characters, please say so in a review. I'm grateful for the time you take to do so.

I have a silly gossipy newsletter called the Chirrup. I promise: no spam, no fowl. (Well, maybe a little wicker fowl and lots of giveaways and sneak peeks.) Find it and more at…

gailcarriger.com

ABOUT THE WRITERBEAST

New York Times bestselling author Gail Carriger (AKA G. L. Carriger) writes to cope with being raised in obscurity by an expatriate Brit and an incurable curmudgeon. She escaped small-town life and inadvertently acquired several degrees in higher learning, a fondness for cephalopods, and a chronic tea habit. She then traveled the historic cities of Europe, subsisting entirely on biscuits secreted in her handbag. She resides in the Colonies, surrounded by fantastic shoes, where she insists on tea imported from London.

Made in the USA
Columbia, SC
03 July 2022